P9-EKX-513

HEARTS *of* AMISH COUNTRY™

PORTRAIT *of* LOVE

Jerry Eicher

Annie's®

AnniesFiction.com

Library of Congress-in-Publication Data
Portrait of Love / by Jerry Eicher
p. cm.
I. Title

2017963685

AnniesFiction.com
(800) 282-6643
Hearts of Amish Country™
Series Creator: Shari Lohner
Series Editor: Shari Lohner

10 11 12 13 14 | Printed in China | 9 8 7 6 5 4 3 2 1

1

The autumn leaves had begun to change in the small Amish community north of Orchard, Nebraska. Yellows and reds brushed with the purples and browns of the season as the world prepared for its winter nap—these colors were the only adornment in the yards of the plain Amish homes.

Wilma Wengerd stepped out on the front porch in the twilight of the early morning to call toward the barn, "Breakfast is ready!"

There was no answer, but she knew the men had their ears tuned. The light in the barn window would dim, and Wilma's *Daett* and her brothers would soon hurry inside, the remainder of their chores left for later. They would gather at the kitchen table for the steaming breakfast of oatmeal, toast, bacon, and eggs she had helped *Mamm* prepare.

Wilma closed her eyes and took a deep breath of the brisk air. Winter would arrive soon, and the roads and fields would be blanketed in white. For the past couple of weeks, the community had been bustling with the activity of fall. The school auction was next week, and Thanksgiving and Christmas lay around the corner. Adding to the excitement, a new family, the Troyers from Wisconsin, planned to move into the area. Ezra and his *Frau*, Lydia, had attended church services a month ago, but most of the community had yet to meet the rest of the family.

There were a dozen Troyer children, her cousin Susie had assured Wilma, though the information had been acquired from unnamed sources. Susie claimed half of them were boys and a couple were even their age. Wilma hugged herself in anticipation. There would be handsome, unmarried men, skilled in farming or carpenter work, in the Troyer family. Perhaps one of them would capture her heart. She certainly could have wed and settled down before with one of the available suitors in their small community. But she wanted the best.

Susie, on the other hand, was ready to settle.

"Clyde Helmuth is close to asking me home on a date," she had told Wilma. "A few more smiles and I know he will."

"You'd best wait. The Troyer family might have better to offer."

She knew Susie would listen to her council. Their Mamms were sisters, and Susie's family lived down the road from Grandpa Byler's place. She would often see Susie at the bakery they managed for Grandpa and Grandma, now that the two were up in years. Grandpa was the bishop of the small community, and he could hold the whole congregation enraptured with his Sunday sermons. He was the rock on which the whole community leaned. He also served as chairman of the school board.

Wilma glanced at the barn as the lights dimmed in the window. She shouldn't daydream on the front porch, even on a lovely, brisk morning. Breakfast was on the table, but there were always last-minute tasks that popped up unexpectedly. She dashed inside.

Mamm smiled at her. "How are things outside?"

"Beautiful. The leaves are at their best with the first morning light. There won't be a cloud in the sky today."

"Sounds like my kind of morning." Mamm motioned to the stairs. "Can you make sure the younger girls are dressed? We don't want Daett waiting for breakfast."

"I'm on my way." Wilma rushed up the old farmhouse stairs.

The kerosene lamp was on in Miriam and Silva's bedroom. The door was open, and her sisters were dressed, but Silva, the youngest, had her *Kapp* askew. Wilma straightened it, then gave them both a quick hug.

"Breakfast smells *goot*," Silva chirped.

"*Yah*, it does," Wilma agreed. "Next week I have to leave at four o'clock for the bakery, so you should get up early to help with the preparations."

"I would now, if you called me," Silva offered.

"It's okay. There will be time to learn your duties later." Wilma ushered them down the stairs.

"Teacher Charity has painted a beautiful horse at school," Miriam said. "I want to paint like her."

Wilma stilled the quick retort that rose to her lips. What Amish girl painted when there were household duties at hand? The schoolteacher had problems, but what else was new? Charity had been a sore subject since Grandpa and the school board had hired her.

The pretty, new teacher from Holmes County, Ohio, had arrived in August, and she initially made quite an impression on the unmarried men. But once Charity's painting habits became known, added to her lack of baking abilities, the attention had begun to wane. Amish men wanted an efficient woman who could handle the gardening, wash the clothes, keep the cellar stocked, fill the pantry, and keep any *Kinner* fed and clean. They didn't need hours wasted applying paint to canvas.

A smirk crept across Wilma's face at the memory of the conversation she had overheard several weeks ago.

"Is this your cake?" Henry Blank had asked Charity at the young folks' Sunday evening supper.

"Yah." Charity had beamed. "I hope you like it. That was the most expensive cake mix I could find at the IGA in Orchard."

Henry had stared, dumbfounded, which was the proper reaction any Amish man should have to a woman who baked from a box.

Miriam tugged on Wilma's arm. "Don't you like Teacher Charity?"

Wilma nearly tripped over the step. "She's nice enough. I'm glad you like her." Criticizing the community's teacher was not her place, but she could have her opinion.

Miriam appeared satisfied with the answer as they entered the kitchen and took their places around the table. Daett was already seated, along with Stephen and Matthew.

"Goot morning, girls," Daett greeted the younger ones. "Everybody is up and cheerful this morning, I see."

Both Miriam and Silva nodded, their smiles crooked.

"Then let us pray and give thanks for the *wunderbah* food Mamm and Wilma have prepared. I'm thinking we won't have Wilma with us for breakfast much longer, now that she's baking cinnamon rolls and sticky buns with Susie down at the bakery. When the news of their offerings spread through the community, I'm sure both will have husbands by Christmas."

Stephen and Matthew joined in the laughter.

Wilma ducked her head as heat crept up her neck. She didn't mind her family's teasing, but she must be careful not to blurt out her hopes concerning the new Troyer family—it wasn't proper. The Lord would reveal what the future held in His time. If she was right, one of the Troyer brothers would be the most handsome and charming man she had ever met.

"Our Father which art in heaven . . ." Daett began to pray.

Wilma envisioned the mysterious Troyer brother driving her home from the hymn singing in his buggy. They would arrive at her house to a kitchen table laden with sticky buns and cinnamon rolls.

"Amen," Daett finished the prayer.

"Amen," Wilma echoed earnestly.

Susie Mast entered the bakery and lit the gas lanterns strung along the ceiling. She blew out the match, then tossed it into the wastebasket.

The sun had risen, but there was still a need for light. She and Wilma must see properly to prepare their baked goods. Grandpa Byler's bakery deserved their best effort. The venture had prospered under Grandpa's guiding hand ever since the young Amish community had put down roots in the area, so there was an established reputation on which they could build and grow. Wilma had agreed to share the responsibility with Susie. Now the future of Plain Rolls & Donuts rested squarely on the shoulders of the two young Amish girls.

Susie put on her apron and glanced out the window. Wilma appeared at the end of the Wengerds' driveway, headed toward the bakery at a brisk pace. They were well matched in so many ways. Both were skilled bakers and hard workers. Wilma would serve the customers while Susie made sure the cupboards were stocked with sufficient amounts of the proper ingredients. Supplies came from the town of O'Neil, two hours away by buggy. Things were done the old-fashioned way in the small community, with hired English drivers used only when necessary.

"Goot morning." Wilma burst through the front door. "Is it not a beautiful day?"

"Goot morning, yourself," Susie returned the greeting with a smile. Her cousin always lifted her spirits.

Wilma took off her coat and leaned conspiratorially toward Susie. "I was thinking this morning about the Troyer family's arrival. I hope you're putting off Clyde and waiting for something better."

A blush crept up Susie's neck. "I am."

Wilma's face glowed. "There should be no competition from Charity. Miriam told me this morning the woman is wrapped up in her paintings."

Susie nodded. "I heard the rumors. Charity is working on a horse painting, and she keeps it covered with a bed linen in her apartment. Are you taking up painting classes, perhaps?"

Wilma snorted in disgust. "You know I wouldn't touch a paintbrush. I don't know the first thing about painting."

"Well, we used to finger paint in school." Susie joined in Wilma's laughter. "Maybe there is still hope for us."

"You're not letting Charity intimidate you, are you?" Horror filled Wilma's voice.

"Not really."

Wilma obviously was not convinced. "There's no reason to be. You run a bakery, and you know our sticky buns are the best. They will capture the unmarried Troyer men's attention. After a month or so, there's not one of them who wouldn't take you home on a date."

"I suppose so. All the same, I came close to accepting Clyde's offer for a ride home on Sunday evening."

"So he asked?" Wilma frowned.

"Yah. I know you are certain there is a better man out there, but I wonder sometimes."

Wilma lifted her chin. "I say wait, even if Clyde Helmuth would make a decent husband."

"I can't stall forever."

"I know you can't, but wait just a couple more weeks until the Troyers arrive. Do you have more details?"

"Just that two of the unmarried men are close to our age."

Wilma clapped her hands in delight. "This is what we have been waiting for—handsome men, charming men, the *best* men. They come from an excellent family. Look at the farm Ezra Troyer purchased—the largest in the community and not far from our bakery. Maybe some of that success will float over and make this bakery boom."

"Grandpa's bakery is already a success," Susie reminded Wilma. "I went over the books with Grandpa last week, and we topped his best sales this past summer. Christmas and Thanksgiving are ahead of us, so we have nothing to worry about."

"I wasn't worried, but we can always do better."

Susie nodded as they busied themselves with mixing the dough for the morning's batch of sticky buns.

As Susie slid the first tray into the oven, Wilma washed her hands in the sink and began to lay out the ingredients for their cinnamon roll recipe.

The front door of the bakery opened while the dough was rising, and Grandpa Byler appeared. "How are my sweet granddaughters this morning?"

Susie smiled, then checked the oven. "I'll have your sticky buns ready in a moment, Grandpa. We got wrapped up in chatting, or we would have had them in the oven already."

He sat down at one of the tables with a sigh. "Nothing like a sticky bun in the early morning to brighten an old man's day."

Wilma gave him a quick peck on the cheek as she rushed past. "What would we do without you?"

His grin split his face. "Those words are sweeter than your sticky buns. You comfort me to the tips of my arthritic toes."

Susie pulled the buns from the oven and carried them over on a platter. "There you are. If you come back later, we'll have fresh cinnamon rolls, but that's it for the moment."

He winked. "The true test of a woman's skills comes from anything she bakes."

"And you know we pass the test each and every day," Wilma hollered from behind the dough-laden table.

"Don't be prideful," Susie scolded her.

"Not prideful," Wilma protested. "Just honest."

"I will keep holding my breath." Grandpa picked up a sticky bun and took a bite. "Perfect! Even your grandma couldn't do better."

"You're not getting another kiss for that," Wilma called out. "Not if you keep us in suspense every morning with your teasing."

Susie studied his bearded face. "You would say they were great even if they weren't, wouldn't you, Grandpa?"

His eyes twinkled. "Now why do we have to spoil a fine morning with suspicions?"

She gave him a hug. "You are the best, Grandpa."

"And so are you," he assured her, reaching for his second sticky bun.

Charity Martin stood by the schoolhouse window watching the small group of children out on the playground. A game of softball had been organized in the short time allotted for the morning recess. Long practice had perfected the exercise so that a full inning could be played before she rang the bell to resume classes. At times, she waited a few minutes longer, but discipline was valued in the community, and tenderness could be perceived as weakness. She was the schoolteacher, and she must act like one.

Grandpa Byler, as everyone called him, had approached her in Holmes County, Ohio, this past summer, along with Millie, his gentle Frau.

"Would you teach for us back in Nebraska?" Grandpa Byler had asked. "We are situated way out west, and nothing much happens, but I think you could do the community goot."

She had almost laughed out loud. What goot could she do anyone? *She* was the broken soul. Grandpa Byler had to know this. The troubles she had caused in Holmes County were no secret. They had culminated in the termination of her engagement to David, Bishop Zook's son. Yet Grandpa Byler had made the offer with kindness in his voice and a smile on his face. Sometimes the far-flung Amish communities were desperate for teachers, but that couldn't have been the only reason she had been offered the position.

Whatever he had known about the uproar her paintings had caused in Bishop Zook's district, he couldn't have known the depth of pain caused by the breakup with David or the agony that still wrenched her heart.

"You will come then," he had said, "after a time spent in prayer about the matter."

And so the decision had been finalized. She *had* prayed. But instead of faith, she found herself living in terror that this chance would vanish into thin air, along with the rest of her hopes and dreams.

Here she was, the community's teacher, accepted apparently, except for her lack of baking skills. The unmarried men's interest in her had waned once that was discovered. Not that she cared. She never wanted to date another man after David. She was thankful that the community tolerated her painting, even if they didn't admire her talent, because she had to continue doing it. She couldn't change who she was. David's Daett had made sure he pounded home that point repeatedly.

"Charity will always be a painter," Bishop Zook had said to his son on the front porch while she shivered beside the buggy. "You are a bishop's son. Perhaps Charity and her paintings have their place in the world, but not in the community."

"But Daett," David had protested in vain.

"You will not marry the girl. I forbid it."

"Even if she plans to stay in the community?" David had asked.

"Charity is not for you!" Bishop Zook had roared. "You need a housewife, a keeper at home, a mother for your Kinner."

"But I love her!" David had finally shouted back.

His words had gone nowhere, and David's disobedience when he continued to date Charity had become a scandal. They were faced with a choice: break up or move to a more liberal community where they could be married.

"Let's do it," David had urged. "There are a dozen English churches in the area who will welcome us with open arms."

She had refused. "I cannot destroy us before we begin. You would never be happy anywhere but in the Amish community."

The torment on his face was answer enough, so the sacrifice had been made. Her dreams torn from their moorings. Their future lost. Their love dead, strangled.

Nothing would change Bishop Zook's mind. She had thought about jumping the fence alone into the English world, removing herself from everything familiar. But the truth was, she wouldn't be happy with a life among the English people, banished from the Amish community. Grandpa Byler's offer had been a way out, a commonsense ending of her continued closeness to the man she wasn't allowed to love.

She slipped into the small apartment attached to the schoolhouse, then opened the door of the back closet. She peeked under the cover of the painting. The wild stallion had taken form this week, his front legs raised to lash out at the world. This was how she remembered David. She had begun the project before Grandpa Byler had invited her to the vast prairies of northern Nebraska.

Charity let the cloth slip from her fingers, then went to ring the bell for the end of recess.

2

A week later, Wilma walked out of the bakery carrying platters of sticky buns. Following her, with one hand free, Susie pulled the door shut. Above them, the blaze of a Nebraska sunset lingered.

Wilma paused to scan the heavens. "We missed most of the sunset, but I guess it was worth it." She admired the goodies in her hands. "Don't they look delicious?"

Susie nodded and balanced the single plate in her hand. "Everyone would still have loved our sticky buns, even if we had taken a few moments to enjoy the sunset."

"Maybe. But we have to make a proper impression tonight. Nothing but the best will do. When the Troyer family arrives, our reputation must precede us."

"What do you suppose Charity will bring to the school auction tonight?" Susie mused.

Wilma lifted her nose in the air. "You know there will be no competition from her."

"Surely Charity won't bring the painting she's been working on."

"I'm guessing she will." Wilma scoffed. "Charity probably thinks her painting is a smashing success. Miriam can't stop chattering about it, and now Silva has joined in. Sounds to me like Charity's on a campaign to win the hearts of the children and, through them, their parents. From there, she plans to recapture the unmarried men's attention. How wrong that woman will be."

"She might bring something baked tonight and surprise us."

Wilma snorted. "What baking can Charity do? Another cake mix from the grocery store in Orchard? The men will laugh her out of Grandpa's barn loft."

"Maybe there is a reason she doesn't have time to stir up a cake from scratch. Teaching can be strenuous, keeping those children straight."

"There are no excuses for baking from a box," Wilma snapped. "But I've heard enough about Charity. Let's do something special tonight to raise extra money for the school."

"Like what? We already baked the best sticky buns we could."

"Not by working harder. Let's tell the auctioneer we'll eat our sticky buns with the highest bidder. You can go with two of the sticky bun plates, and I will go with the other two."

Susie paled. "You would dare? What if no one bids?"

"The men will love the chance to court us." Wilma grinned. "Can't you see Clyde paying over $100 for the chance to eat sticky buns with you right there at the school auction?"

Susie took a deep breath. "You and your nerve!"

Wilma raised her plates higher in salute. "To a two-hundred-dollar bid with us on the ticket and an unforgettable evening for the cousins."

Susie's smile was thin. "You do have a way of encouraging the faint of heart."

"You have plenty of courage. You are the heart and soul of our bakery business. I wouldn't know how to run things without you and Grandpa. You're the one who understands him when he talks numbers and figures."

"You take care of the really important things. You talk with the customers. We have a great product, but your charm has every English housewife from twenty miles around visiting our bakery."

"May my charm extend to the men tonight!" Wilma gave one last flourish of her sticky bun plates. "What a great evening this will be."

They approached Grandpa Byler's barn, where a line of buggies was already parked along the fencerow. From all appearances, there would be a record attendance for the evening's events. Even a few English automobiles were parked near Grandpa's house, and several more were in the process of turning into the lane.

Wilma paused to catch her breath. "What if an English man bids on our sticky buns?"

Susie came to an abrupt halt. "We can't do this."

"Yah, we can." Wilma thumped Susie on the arm. "We can eat with an English man."

"We could tell the auctioneer that only Amish men can bid."

Wilma shook her head. "Better that we use the pressure to our advantage. This might cause the Amish men to bid even higher. Smile at any English man who bids on our sticky buns. We might get a $500 bid. Perhaps two of them? That would be $1,000 raised for the school fund! Never has this happened in the history of the community."

"That is something like counting your chickens before they hatch."

"We must be bold and brave! Think of the school fund," Wilma declared. "We will succeed. We can't pass up a chance like this. By the next school auction, our hands might be claimed in marriage to one of the Troyers, and this glorious opportunity will have slipped away." She smiled and marched forward with her plates of sticky buns held high.

An hour later, Susie pressed her way through the crowd gathered for the school auction. Her plates of sticky buns had been deposited among the other baked goods the community women had brought to sell.

Their offering appeared small and insignificant from a distance, surrounded by cinnamon rolls, cherry pies, and baked apple crisp. Smaller farming implements, donated by English stores in Orchard, were laid out on an adjoining table. A beautiful Texas Star quilt the community women had finished last week was the centerpiece set against the far barn wall. Everyone had given something and poured their heart into the effort. School was a vital part of the community, and financing the parochial institution brought out the best in everyone.

Susie jumped when a man's voice spoke at her shoulder. "Are those your sticky buns on the table over there?"

Susie whirled around and faced Clyde. "Yah, I . . . uh . . . we brought them."

His smile warmed Susie's heart. "You don't have to be modest. Mamm said our English neighbor purchased some last week and couldn't stop talking about the superb quality and the baking abilities of our Amish women. That would be you, right?"

"We baked them together," Susie explained. "Wilma and I."

"There are four plates, two apiece." Clyde moved closer. "I saw Wilma talking with the auctioneer earlier. If I know Wilma, she was whispering special instructions, perhaps some trick up her sleeve."

"You should ask her," Susie told him.

Clyde bent low and whispered, "Please tell me. I want a chance to buy them."

She gave him a sweet smile. "We will eat the sticky buns with the man who makes the purchase."

"Right here in front of everyone?" His face glowed.

"That could come at a considerable price," she teased.

"But it's all for a goot cause. And I would get to eat with you. Let everyone know my intentions."

"I'm making no promises," Susie warned, "but the auctioneer will mention which plates go with Wilma or me."

Clyde didn't appear to hear, walking away as if in a daze.

They might have gotten in deeper than either of them had intended, but it was too late to back out now.

Susie noticed Charity standing against the back wall of the barn, surrounded by a group of her students. They were looking at something, but she couldn't see what it was from this distance.

Susie moved closer. The painting! Charity had indeed brought it. Susie caught her breath as she studied the beautiful picture. A wild roan stallion pawed the sky while prairie grass flowed into the distance. Strength and muscle combined in the horse's limbs to bring the animal to life. Charity knew what she was doing. But this was an Amish school auction. How much money would the painting bring?

Abner Kauffman, the auctioneer, stepped up to the raised platform. Grandpa had allowed the young Amish man to attend evening classes at the nearest community college so he could pass the state exam and earn his credentials. Abner explained the general purpose of the evening before he began to chatter away. The man had a nice rhythm with his singsong voice. Things started selling at a rapid clip and at a decent price.

"We have a very special treat tonight," Abner called out thirty minutes later. "Sticky buns from our local bakery that come with an even more special opportunity. Miss Wilma Wengerd and Miss Susie Mast, cousins from right here in the community, will share their baked goods with the highest bidder. Now, young men, who can pass that up? Who knows where a few dollars invested tonight could lead? Perhaps to a brighter future, though with empty pockets, I would guess. These sticky buns will not go cheap."

Laughter rippled through the audience.

Abner chanted away, and the bidding started for Wilma's two plates.

"Come on, boys," Abner encouraged. "Let's not be shy about this. We know that a woman who can bake sticky buns like this could also warm a heart with goot food on any cold winter day."

The bid quickly climbed from $100 to $300.

"Now, there we go, boys," Abner said. "That's what I'm talking about."

An English man joined in the bidding.

"Now, how can our local boys allow this?" Abner teased. "Somebody better get with it, or we will lose one of our pretty maidens to the outside competition."

The bid shot up and settled in at $650. Susie had thought Wilma's hope for $500 for two plates of sticky buns was quite high, but $650 was outrageous.

Abner goaded and begged, but the number wouldn't budge. "Sold," he hollered. "To myself for $700. I'll claim my prize after I'm through with the sale."

Laughter came from the crowd.

Abner moved on to Susie's offering. "Now for our second plate with the same deal. And I'm not buying. I can't date both of these girls at the same time. Imagine what their fathers would say, to say nothing of their grandfather, our own dear bishop! So help me out here."

It began at $400, with the English man making the opening bid.

Susie tried to breathe evenly. Would Clyde be able to keep up?

Clyde waved his hand and didn't stop until a bid of $600 was reached, at which point the other bidders gave up.

"Sold!" Abner yelled. "To Clyde Helmuth, who will now enjoy his sweet treat with Susie Mast."

Someone pounded Clyde on the back as he went to claim his plates of sticky buns.

Susie sat down at a small table set up for the event and waited. "You paid $600," she scolded when he arrived.

"You are worth every penny," Clyde replied.

Her hands shook as she took the plate from him to open the wrapper. Carefully she picked up a bun and held it out to him.

Their fingers brushed as Clyde accepted the bun from her. He grinned broadly as he took a bite, clearly thinking she'd touched him on purpose.

Susie took a piece of sticky bun for herself. She bit into it, but she couldn't taste a thing. Wilma's idea had brought in a huge amount of money for the school, but Susie feared there might be unintended consequences. What those consequences might be, she wasn't sure. But this didn't feel goot.

Charity slipped to the back of the crowd as Abner stopped next to her painting. Wilma and Susie had made quite a splash earlier with their offer to eat sticky buns with the highest bidder. Both girls had clearly endeared themselves to the unmarried men of the community.

Not that Charity wanted another relationship after David, but why couldn't she bake? She had tried often while growing up at home, but she had always been drawn away from Mamm's recipes by the lure of painting. What was a recipe for sticky buns but a collection of flour tossed together with eggs and sugar? An Amish first grader could make sticky buns, yet she couldn't. The fact was clearly not lost on the men of the Amish community. Abner still wore a wide grin from claiming his prize, and Clyde was still chatting with Susie.

Why could no one understand that art like hers was a rarer skill than baking? Maybe there was a man or a woman in the crowd who did. She needed one such person tonight to pay a decent price for the stallion, and then her honor would be redeemed.

Charity shouldn't have taken the risk, but she had nothing else of value to offer. The painting would bring well over $1,000 back at the little gift shop in Holmes County. Of course, that was why she was here and why her heart ached relentlessly day after day.

"And now we have a painting," Abner declared. "Let's see—a stallion, I think, rearing toward the heavens. How about that?"

One of the bearded community men came up and whispered in Abner's ear.

"Okay!" Abner announced once the man had moved away. "This painting is brought to us by our schoolteacher, Miss Charity Martin, so let's begin."

No one moved to bid. Looking around, Charity noticed that her usual customers, the English, seemed to be gone.

"Come on," Abner urged, but clearly his mind was not on the painting. He kept gazing at Wilma in the front row.

A dollar was bid, and Charity sat down. She couldn't hide, but at least no one could see her as easily. *A dollar? One dollar!* She wanted to scream and never stop.

"Five, a five," Abner chanted. "We can do better than that, boys, for our bright, young teacher."

Charity clasped her hands until her fingernails dug into her palms.

"Sold," Abner hollered a moment later, "to Grandpa Byler for ten dollars. You got yourself a painting there, Bishop, and a pretty one at that."

Charity forced herself to stand and slipped out of the barn. In the darkness, she covered her face with both hands. Sobs racked her body as she stumbled across the field.

3

The week after the school auction, Wilma peered out the bakery window at the Troyers' empty farmhouse. Behind her, the wooden tables were spread with bread, cinnamon rolls, and sticky buns. Those would likely be sold by noon, but she hadn't raised the daily quota yet. Scarcity had its allure, and day-old sticky buns did not meet the high standards of Plain Rolls & Donuts.

Wilma smiled through the window glass. The memory lingered of Abner Kauffman sitting close to her at the school auction. She had enjoyed her time with him. Abner had sat there smacking his lips in delight, sneaking glances at her. The man would have asked her for a date if she hadn't chattered on about another subject every time the conversation left an opening. Abner had wisely taken the cue and dropped the matter for the time being.

Could she find a better husband than Abner? Wilma pursed her lips and imagined handsome men moving furniture into the Troyers' house. Susie seemed ready to settle for Clyde, but settling wasn't in Wilma's heart. There was something better out there, even if Susie didn't agree. One of the unmarried Troyer men would surely be the answer.

"You shouldn't do that. It's not decent." Susie's voice behind her made Wilma jump.

"I'm not doing anything. I'm waiting for the Troyer family to arrive."

"Someone on the road might see you senselessly staring at an empty house."

Wilma smiled again. "The Troyer brothers may be exactly what we have been waiting for. Just think. Our Kinner would be double cousins!"

"They would be double cousins if we were sisters, but we're not," Susie corrected her. "Anyway, I'm not making my biggest life decision for such reasons."

"Well, we're almost like sisters." Wilma checked on the cinnamon rolls cooling on the table. "At least you won't have to worry about Charity when the Troyer family arrives."

"And neither do you have to worry about Charity when it comes to Abner."

"We shouldn't quarrel." Wilma carefully drizzled thick icing over the rolls, making sure to press the gooey sweetness into each crevice. She drew a deep breath over the plate. The delicious smell warmed her heart.

"So where will things go from here?"

Wilma gestured to the sticky buns with a flourish. "The Troyer brothers arrive, and we seal the deal with a demonstration of our baking skills."

"Are you sure Charity doesn't know them?"

Wilma whirled around. "Why do you ask that?"

"Just wondering. Most people have relatives in Holmes County, Ohio. Maybe the Troyers visited and they have met?"

"But that's not possible."

"Anything is possible."

"So Charity would have her foot in the door?"

"It would explain why she took the chance with her painting at the school auction, knowing how the community feels about such things."

A chill ran up Wilma's back. "Enough of that. I know I'm right."

Susie tilted her head. "But you don't know."

"I don't *know*, but there is a simple explanation for how Charity acted at the auction. The girl still thinks she can win over the men with her painting skills. But you wait and see. She'll have to learn that the old ways are alive and well in this community."

Susie waved her hand dismissively as she glanced out the window. "The Troyers are here."

Wilma dashed to the window, and Susie joined her a moment later. Together they peered down the road, where a large moving truck was turning into the Troyers' driveway.

"There go Grandpa and Grandma to help." Susie motioned to the two forms walking slowly toward the Troyers' house. "It looks like Grandma made a casserole to share for lunch."

"We should go," Wilma declared.

"And leave the bakery like this?"

"We have to go as soon as we can," she insisted.

"I agree, but we can't go right this minute." Susie stared at Wilma as if she had lost her mind.

"But we must soon." Wilma couldn't think straight now that the Troyer family had arrived.

The doorbell dinged, and one of their regular English customers, Mrs. Wright, walked in.

"Goot morning," Wilma sang out.

"And good morning to you too," Mrs. Wright replied with a bright smile. "I see I caught the bread while it's still fresh from the oven."

Baking that brings such a smile to Mrs. Wright's face must melt the heart of any Amish man, Wilma reasoned as she rushed forward to serve the woman. *Surely Susie and I have nothing to worry about from Charity, whether the Troyers already know her or not.*

At ten thirty Susie opened the bakery door and glanced up and down the road. No customers in sight. "We have a few moments," she hollered back to Wilma.

"We're going even if someone is coming," Wilma replied, her arms filled with cinnamon rolls and bread. "Grab the sticky bun plates."

Susie hid her smile. "You're going to let *me* carry them?"

"You won't drop them. And they'll know we both made them because *we* are Plain Rolls & Donuts and we're known for our goot baking."

"I'm putting up a sign." Susie found a blank piece of paper under the counter. With a black marker she wrote, *Closed until* . . .

Wilma peered at the paper. "Eleven thirty. We need at least that much time."

Susie wrote the suggested time. They could always come back sooner. Wilma assumed a lot about the new arrivals. There was a chance neither of the cousins would be interested in the Troyer brothers or the brothers in them. However, Wilma was usually right. Susie taped the sign on the door and gathered up the two plates of sticky buns.

"Grandpa and Grandma just went past on their way home," Wilma said as Susie closed the door.

"Didn't you want Grandpa there when we deliver the baked items?"

Wilma made a face. "Grandpa understands. Any girl would want to make a goot impression on new arrivals."

"This is still a little bold, don't you think?"

"Take courage." Wilma marched down the road with her head held high. "Let's show the Troyer brothers what the cousins can bake."

Susie hurried to keep up. She had no doubt they would make a proper impression with their baking, but if Clyde heard of their visit, would he understand? Surely Clyde would know that neighbors must be welcomed into the community. If there really was competition, she would deal with that later. Wilma was right. They should avail themselves of every opportunity to find the best husbands.

Wilma slowed as they approached the Troyers' residence and ducked her head in a less prideful posture. Wilma could breathe fire, but she also knew when to tame the flame.

Susie waited as Wilma knocked on the front door.

The gray-haired Lydia answered. "Goot morning, girls."

"We are from the bakery down the road," Wilma chirped. "This is Susie, and I'm Wilma."

"Welcome to the community," Susie added. "I hope things are going well with the move."

"Oh, indeed they are," Lydia answered. "The community has gone out of its way to make us feel welcome, and now you have brought bread and cinnamon rolls."

"And Susie has sticky buns, our specialty." Wilma beamed.

"They look delicious." Lydia's smile was warm. "I guess you know who we are—Ezra and Lydia Troyer. Did we meet you at church?"

"Yes. There were a lot of people when you visited," Wilma said.

"Then we must get acquainted. Please come in."

Susie and Wilma stepped inside.

"Let me take your things." Lydia reached for Wilma's baked goods.

"We can set them on the kitchen table," Wilma said.

"I'm sure your bakery is waiting for you in the middle of the day."

"It's not a bother," Wilma insisted. "Your day is the one filled to the brim with the move."

"That is true." Lydia stepped aside and motioned for them to follow.

Susie nodded to the community men who wrestled with a piece of furniture halfway up the stairs. At least Clyde wasn't among them. But where were the Troyer brothers?

"Right here." Lydia paused at the kitchen table. Several pies and a casserole already sat invitingly in the center. "Deacon Jonas's Frau, Ann, brought the pies, and Bishop Byler's Frau, Millie, made the casserole. They seem like such kind people."

"They are." Wilma set down her cinnamon rolls and bread. "The Bylers are our grandparents."

"Oh, I should have guessed. You are just like them." Lydia took the plates of sticky buns from Susie. "We'll get everyone straight before long."

"Of course," Susie assured her.

She nudged Wilma toward the door, not wanting to overstay their welcome.

Lydia stopped them with a laugh. "Here I am talking about getting to know everyone, and I don't even introduce my family."

Susie held her breath as Lydia led them back into the living room.

"This is Lucie and baby Wendell." Lydia motioned to the back of the room where a little girl sat on a blanket on the floor cradling a baby in her arms.

"Hi," Susie and Wilma said in unison.

Lucie responded with a shy smile.

Ezra emerged from another room with two young men close behind.

"This is Ezra. You saw him at church," Lydia said. "And James and Amos, our two oldest." She nodded at the cousins. "Wilma and Susie run the bakery down the road. Their grandmother brought the casserole we will have for lunch today."

Susie tried to breathe. James and Amos were square-jawed and more handsome than any men the community could boast. How had Wilma known?

"Goot to meet you." James shook Susie's hand.

Then Amos took her hand and appeared to study her face. "Did Mamm say you have a bakery? Did you happen to bring samples?"

"Amos!" Lydia chided.

Amos grinned and patted his stomach. "Sorry. I'm just starved."

"Same here," James joined in. "You girls look like you could cook up a dinner worthy of any Amish table."

"We hope so." Wilma dropped her gaze. "Our humble offerings are in the kitchen."

"I'm sure we'll be seeing more of you, then." James had a twinkle in his eye.

"We'll be at church on Sunday." Wilma peered up at him through her lashes and smiled.

Susie reached for Wilma's arm and led the way out.

"The conversation had barely begun," Wilma whispered on the front porch.

"They didn't need us to stay long," Susie whispered back. "They're busy."

Wilma didn't appear to hear. "We made an awesome impression. Amos almost fainted gazing at your beautiful face. Wait till they bite into our sticky buns and our cinnamon rolls. Charity doesn't stand a chance with her paintings."

Susie stilled her protest. She was a little dizzy from her encounter with Amos. Was it possible that he had been impressed with her? Her heart pounded at the thought. Was the conquest of such a handsome and charming man even possible?

Wilma hummed a happy tune as they walked along. They entered the bakery, and the sight of Grandpa Byler on a stepladder stopped them.

"Grandpa!" Wilma exclaimed. "What are you doing?"

He faced them, a big smile on his face. Then he motioned to Charity's painting, hanging front and center on their bakery wall. The rearing stallion reached toward the heavens in a glorious splash of color. "I thought this would be the perfect place for such a beautiful painting. Don't you agree?"

After school had closed for the day, Charity drove her buggy over to the home of the new arrivals. Several of the Troyer children would be attending school in the morning, and she thought a friendly visit might make their transition to their new class easier. She had met Ezra and Lydia when they visited the community a month ago, but she had yet to meet the rest of the family.

Charity pulled into the driveway and parked her buggy beside the large, red barn. She climbed down to tie her horse and approached the house. She took the porch steps one at a time and knocked on the door.

It opened to reveal the smiling face of Lydia Troyer. "Goot evening. You are the teacher, yah?"

Charity's greeting stuck in her throat. Why was she overcome with bashfulness?

Ezra's bearded face appeared behind Lydia, and he offered his hand. "Nice of you to stop by. Becky will appreciate it." He laughed. "Samuel and Jonathon weren't worried, but Becky was in a tizzy. Go call her, Lydia."

Lydia hurried off.

Ezra regarded Charity carefully. "So you're from Holmes County."

"Yah," Charity choked out. "This is my first term teaching here."

"That's what I heard." He seemed satisfied after his scrutiny. "Bishop Byler spoke highly of you. It sounds like he was personally involved in your hiring. If Bishop Byler approves of your teaching, I approve too."

"I hope he does." Her voice still didn't work properly.

Ezra studied her again. "Bishop Byler says you paint."

Charity felt dizzy, and she held on to the doorframe. Would her paintings continue to haunt her in this out-of-the-way place? If only she could stop painting . . . but she couldn't.

Before Charity could answer, a young girl joined them.

"Here's Becky." Ezra smiled, appearing to forget his painting question. He gave his daughter a one-armed hug. "This is your new teacher."

Charity stepped closer to extend her hand. "Welcome to the community. I hope to see you tomorrow in school."

A shy smile crept across Becky's face as she shook Charity's hand. "I am happy that you stopped by."

"So am I," Charity said. "I'll see you then." She smiled at them and walked away quickly.

Two handsome young men came out of the barn.

Charity assumed they wanted to help her turn the buggy around. But she untied her horse and shook the reins before they reached her, then whirled out of the driveway.

4

The next morning, Wilma unlocked the bakery door and took in the sight of dawn stretching red and yellow tendrils across the horizon. On the walk from home, she had taken her time, drinking in the glorious sight. Surely this was a sign from heaven that her fears of the night had been for nothing. Life would go on as it should with things operating in their proper place. Charity's painting would not affect their business, even if Grandpa had decided to display the stallion prominently on the bakery wall.

Wilma allowed herself a small smile at the Troyers' place. The house was silhouetted against the sky with the light of a kerosene lamp flickering in the kitchen window. The soft glow was a vision of loveliness against the bursting dawn. The simple things in life were such a comfort.

Wilma's gaze moved to the barn. The outlines of farm animals could be seen in the barnyard, but no light was evident in the windows. James and Amos must be busy with the morning chores, even if she couldn't see the glow of their lantern. The brothers' memory of the sticky buns they had eaten yesterday must still linger, even in the hustle and bustle of their moving day. She imagined the baked goods had given the brothers pleasant dreams last night.

"Stop staring at their place," Susie said from behind her.

Wilma jumped. "I need pleasant thoughts this morning after worrying all night about that painting on our wall."

"I know." Susie sighed. "Grandpa must have his reasons. And it is beautiful."

Wilma watched the horizon for another moment before letting the comment go. "I think the Troyer brothers are still contemplating our baking skills. That's what will win the day."

"Everyone likes our sticky buns." Susie entered the bakery. "Is Charity getting to you? Remember that there is no competition."

Wilma ignored the remark as she followed her inside. "They liked us yesterday. I know they did."

Susie glanced at the painting hanging on the wall. "Do you admit it's beautiful?"

"I'm admitting nothing. It's there because Grandpa likes it."

"Maybe our customers will buy more goodies under the shadow of a nice painting."

"Painting and baking have *nothing* in common." Wilma glared at the painting before measuring out the flour and retrieving the milk jug from the refrigerator.

Today was doughnut day, which took extra work, so they prepared the delicacies only twice a week. Maybe they could use the doughnuts as an excuse to visit the Troyers again. They could offer the family something extra for lunch. She might just dare take the chance.

Wilma paused at the sound of footsteps in the driveway outside. "Grandpa?"

"Must be. It's too early for customers."

The door swung open, and the Troyer brothers peeked in.

"Anybody home?" James called out.

Wilma rushed forward. "Goot morning." She made no attempt to hide her flour-covered hands.

"We nearly died from a stomachache last night," Amos deadpanned. "We had to come down and see if we could find the culprits."

"Surely not!" Susie exclaimed, a deep blush coloring her cheeks.

"Amos is teasing," Wilma told her. "They loved our offerings. Am I right?"

The brothers both grinned and laughed.

"Amos and I divided the last cinnamon roll at suppertime," James said. "That was some amazing baking, if you ask me."

"Which is quite an opinion." Amos winked. "My brother is an expert at evaluating cooking."

James chuckled. "I simply enjoy goot food. What is wrong with that?"

"Nothing at all," Wilma said. "Our bakery depends on people with goot taste."

"Ching, ching," Amos teased. "She's fleecing you already."

Wilma gasped. "Of course you aren't paying. I was referring to our English customers. You two can have all the baked goodies you want anytime. Just stop by."

James laughed. "I might just take you up on that. Being in a large family means we lack those kinds of treats. Mamm and our sisters only have time for the basics most days. So thanks for the food you brought yesterday."

"We could have stopped in on our way home from work to thank you," Amos said, "but it didn't seem right to wait."

"Where are you working?" Susie leaped into the conversation.

"Daett has a carpentry job lined up in Orchard," James replied.

"You are carpenters?" Susie's voice was filled with awe. "Most men around here are farmers."

"Daett taught us." Amos glanced around the bakery. He pointed at the picture. "Where did you get that?"

"Our grandpa hung the painting," Wilma said. "I guess he has goot taste."

James contemplated the picture. "I'm not an expert, but Amos and I do enjoy the arts. That painting looks almost professional."

"It is so lifelike. That's some feat. I wonder who the artist is." Amos walked closer and scanned the surface. "It's signed CLM."

James stared at his brother. "That painting of the waterfalls in Holmes County that we saw in a shop near Berlin, Ohio, was done by CLM."

Amos snapped his fingers. "It was. The young English cashier told us she thought the painter's name was Charity. How would your grandfather have acquired a painting by this same person—if it is the same person?"

"Our schoolteacher, Charity, painted it," Susie said.

"But that's not possible." Amos gaped at her. "She's Amish."

"Do you know Charity's full name?" James asked.

"It's Martin," Wilma said. "I don't know her middle name. Most Amish don't have them." She could just sink through the floor. How could these perfect men be interested in Charity's painting? Her worst nightmare was coming true.

"And most Amish girls can't paint like that!" James studied the painting again.

"Let me get you something to eat before you go. We don't have anything fresh, but there are cinnamon rolls from yesterday." Wilma raced to the walk-in cupboard and returned with a wrapped bag. "Here!"

"The whole bag?" Amos asked.

Wilma's smile was frozen in place. "For your lunch."

"Thank you," they said in unison.

"But we didn't come for food," James assured her, obviously still distracted by the painting on the wall.

"We know, but stop in on your way home, and we'll have doughnuts for you."

James laughed. "Mamm will scold us for taking these. We don't want our parents to forbid us from stopping by your bakery."

Wilma made herself join in their laughter, but the effort hurt.

"Thanks again," Amos said and followed his brother out the door.

"They liked Charity's painting," Susie moaned. "What are we going to do?"

"We will bake the best doughnuts the community can produce," Wilma said, her voice resolute. "That will make them forget about Charity's painting. Look how quickly they forgot about it when I brought out that bag of cinnamon rolls, and those were a day old. Fresh-baked goodies win every day of the week."

"You were wrong about Charity not knowing the Troyer family."

"They know of her. I will admit that."

"What do you think the *L* stands for in Charity's name?"

Wilma didn't answer as she gave the painting a long, fierce glare.

The late-afternoon sun blazed through the west windows of the bakery as Susie busied herself cleaning the last of the grease from the oven. Doughnut day was exhausting enough without the tension the Troyer brothers had brought with them this morning.

Susie paused in her work when Wilma walked over with a plate of doughnuts.

"Why did you keep those? We could have sold them."

"And have none when the Troyer brothers appear? We would lose our advantage."

"We don't have an advantage. Not with Charity's painting on the wall—or Charity in the community, for that matter."

"Forget that awful painting," Wilma snapped. "Spend your time thinking about how we can entertain the brothers next week. We should plan some event where we can display our goot baking."

"I thought they were coming by tonight."

"They will." Wilma lifted her chin high. "But we must continue the effort, and the more public the better. Charity needs to see them eating and enjoying our delicacies."

"I think you are going too far."

"Think. *Think!*" Wilma waved her hand about, nearly upsetting the plate of doughnuts.

"Careful!"

Wilma's hand still waved in the air. "I have an idea. We could schedule a cornhusking party at Grandpa's next week. His sweet corn is about ready, and the young folks could help with the harvest."

Susie glanced at the dirty bakery floor. "Instead of planning more work, you should help me. We have two hours of cleaning before the bakery is ready for tomorrow morning."

"They're here." Wilma nearly tripped in her dash to the front door.

Happy chatter filled the bakery as Wilma met James and Amos and ushered them inside. Her face glowed. "I knew you were coming. We kept a plate of doughnuts especially for you."

"Hi." Amos smiled at Susie. "We didn't mean to cause extra work, but we couldn't pass up your offer. Not after a hard day's work."

James grabbed a doughnut and wolfed it down in two bites. "Heavenly! Absolutely heavenly!"

Amos ate slower, but he was soon on his second one.

"More?" Wilma offered with a hopeful expression.

James laughed. "I've already spoiled my supper, but after the awful mess we had to tear out today on the construction site, this comforts the body and the soul. Remodeling isn't the easiest work, but there is satisfaction at the end of the process."

"Nothing more satisfying than these doughnuts." Amos eyed his third.

Wilma held out the plate.

Amos winked as he took another doughnut. "These are so goot."

Susie looked away. Her face would soon be bright red from the brothers' praise.

Wilma obviously had no such compunctions. She shoved the plate in James's direction. "Have another, and while you do, let me tell you about the cornhusking party we are planning for next week, right here at Grandpa's place. You two are the first to receive invitations."

"How fun." James appeared pleased.

"It's for all the young folks, so you have to come." Wilma batted her eyes at him.

"Do I get more doughnuts?" James teased.

"I'll make sure there are a dozen especially for you," Wilma promised.

They laughed and Susie joined in. The Troyers would be at the cornhusking party, with or without doughnuts.

"Thank you again," they said together and hurried out the door.

"See!" Wilma declared. "What did I tell you? Not once did they notice the painting."

Susie glanced up at the picture. What did the middle initial stand for in Charity's name? She would never dare to ask. In the meantime, there was the bakery to clean.

That evening, after a meager supper of bread with deli ham and a tossed salad, Charity lit the gas lantern in her apartment. The soft glow filled the interior. She glanced at the closet. Painting placed a strain on the eyes even in bright sunlight. She should save her painting for the daylight hours, but there was always schoolwork waiting then.

She had to paint, even with the misery it had already brought her. Charity cleared the table to bring out the wooden frame. She had stretched the canvas tight over the frame yesterday evening when the first urges of inspiration had stirred.

The Lord is my shepherd. The familiar words from Psalm 23 danced in her head. *I shall not want.*

Yet she desperately wanted David's arms around her, with his tender kisses brushing her cheeks and forehead. They had spent many Sunday evening hours cuddled on the living room couch of the Martins' home in Holmes County. So close to each other then, but now separated by cruel fate.

Charity uncapped the paint tray and gripped the brush. She would forget those times with David somehow. She must think instead of a shepherd reaching out his hands, his sheep below him, with a stream in the distance, the grass tall and plentiful. That scene must have been done a thousand times, yet the beauty was still there, expressing the longing of the human heart for comfort. And every artist put his or her own special touches into it, as she would do.

She steadied her hand and moved the brush slowly and deliberately. David was probably dating another girl by this time. A handsome man like him would find plenty of girls eager to return his affections. His smile would warm another heart while she had only a cold brush in her hand. She painted because she had nothing left. Maybe this had always been the truth. Bishop Zook might have made the best judgment of his life when he forbade the marriage of his son to a foolish artist.

Charity turned her face away from the canvas. She had to stop this. She had to move on. But how? Would her life be nothing but teaching and painting? Would there be no love of a man? Would she be punished double for having known a man's sweet affection?

She must believe otherwise, or she would lose her mind. She must see kindness in the face of the shepherd. She must trust His desire to lead her away from loneliness and despair. Her grief was a desert, but the oasis lay somewhere.

Charity squared her shoulders and faced the painting. She would paint a shepherd leading his sheep through the desert, with the lush waters in the distance. The brush moved faster as the gas lantern hummed its high-pitched song.

5

The last glow of sunset hung above the young people gathered at Grandpa Byler's cornhusking party. Wilma paused in the rows of tall stalks to gaze skyward. James and Amos had arrived in their buggy ten minutes ago. They were in the cornfield somewhere, but a rushed greeting would not be proper. She had no claim on James—yet.

She reached for another ear of corn. She twisted it off the stalk and tossed the green bundle into the small wagon parked between the rows of corn. Susie had watched the Troyer brothers arrive, then made a beeline to Grandpa's basement, where ice cream was being made. Susie needed more confidence, but she was doing her part in her own way. Regardless, Clyde and Abner were history.

Wilma smiled. The homemade ice cream would be served with the doughnuts and cinnamon rolls they had worked so hard to bake this morning. The effort had been worth the pain. She was tired, but deliriously happy. The Troyers would be suitably impressed with their baked goods, and any lingering memory of Charity's painting in the recesses of their minds would be gone.

"How are you, Wilma?" A man's voice spoke behind her.

Wilma jumped.

Clyde cleared his throat. "Sorry. I didn't mean to startle you."

She gave him a friendly smile. "Just watching the sunset. I guess I got caught up in the glories the Lord placed in the sky."

He nodded distractedly. It was clear that was not why he'd approached her. "Where's Susie?"

"In the basement, helping with the ice cream making."

He grunted. "Did you girls by any chance supply the baked goodies tonight?"

"Now why would you ask such a question?" Wilma tried to tease.

"I still haven't forgotten what those sticky buns cost me at the school auction. You owe me a lot of baked goods."

Wilma made a face at him. "You know that talking with Susie was well worth it."

Clyde huffed. "There's no question the woman can bake—unless you do the baking and Susie handles the business end."

Wilma patted Clyde's arm. "You don't have to worry. Susie bakes right by my side, and we did bring the doughnuts and cinnamon rolls tonight. But don't you think someone else might have noticed?"

Clyde's face grew grim. "Are you trying to tell me something?"

Wilma removed another ear of corn. "What I'm saying is that if things don't work out between Susie and you, there is always Charity." She motioned to Charity's buggy, which had just pulled into Grandpa's driveway.

"You know who I want," Clyde said, his voice low.

"Sometimes we can't get what we want." Wilma's gaze lingered on Charity standing beside her horse. Grandpa had come out of the barn to help her unhitch. The problem was that James had admired Charity's paintings, and the bitterness threatened to seep into the joy of the evening. Wilma had to believe the matter would soon be resolved. James would ask her home on a date.

"Goot evening," Clyde said to someone behind her.

Wilma whirled around.

"Glad to see me?" Abner grinned down at her.

"I'm off to the basement." Clyde moved away through the tall cornstalks.

"I'm not competition, am I?" Abner teased, but he didn't appear worried.

"Hi." Wilma forced herself to speak.

"Is that all the greeting I get?" he protested. "Must I chant a line or two? Sell off a few ears of corn?"

Wilma gave him a weak smile. "I don't think that will be necessary. You are handsome enough, even when you're not auctioneering."

Abner's face glowed. "Now that's what I need—words of praise from a beautiful woman."

"You are so full of yourself."

He roared with laughter. "Are you eating with me tonight?"

"You paid for only one meal."

"I thought that price at the auction would buy me a month of meals."

They laughed.

"I hear there are free doughnuts tonight," a nearby man chimed in. "Having regrets, Abner?"

"Spending time with Wilma was worth every penny." Abner punched the man playfully on the arm. "And the school benefited. On top of that, you can't find better baking anywhere in the community."

"There are other excellent cooks in the community."

The men moved farther down the row of corn, and Abner followed them. "Don't worry. I know he's wrong about that. See you later," he said over his shoulder to Wilma.

She didn't answer. She wanted James to sit with her tonight while they sampled homemade ice cream and ate cinnamon rolls and doughnuts. He was out here in the cornfield somewhere. Dusk had fallen, and the lanterns would soon be set up inside the barn. There were only a few stalks left in her row, and the little wagon spilled over with green ears of corn. If James appeared, they could wheel the wagon into the barn together. She would pull while James pushed. The message would be sent to Abner and anyone else who wished to notice—especially Charity. James was taken. She would have staked her claim.

Wilma tossed in the last ear of corn and reached for the wagon tongue.

Abner rushed toward her. "Thought I'd forgotten you? I don't expect a girl to lug in the wagon by herself."

Wilma pretended to concentrate on pulling. She didn't want to enter the barn with Abner helping her. James would see, and he would read it the wrong way. James might even remember Charity's beautiful painting hanging on their bakery wall.

"There we go," Abner announced as they burst into the lantern light inside Grandpa's barn.

Rows of chairs had been set up along the outside walls with a pile of green corn ears in the center. Already a few of the young people were hard at work. They stripped the husk to expose the creamy yellow of the sweet corn inside and tossed the ears into water-filled metal tubs for their first cleaning.

Wilma forced herself to smile. "We can sit over there." Abner had paid plenty to eat with her at the school auction. She could give him another evening.

Down in Grandpa's basement, Susie stepped back as Clyde slowly cranked the handle on the ice cream maker. He had appeared ten minutes ago and insisted on helping. She should be honored that Clyde had sought her out when there were more exciting things going on in Grandpa's barn. The young people gathered inside would be chatting merrily while they removed the husks from the ears of corn.

Few things could match the joy of such an evening, and she was happy—only she wasn't. That was the problem. She should be happy that Clyde was here, and she would be, but for the Troyer brothers. How *wunderbah* it would have been if Amos had noticed her.

"Think it's ready?" Clyde asked.

"Let me see." Susie reached for the handle.

"You can't turn it," he warned, straightening his back.

True to Clyde's words the handle barely budged under the pressure she applied with both hands.

Clyde grinned. "Shall I carry this out to the barn?"

"We might as well. I'll get a bowl and spoon upstairs."

"Let the other girls bring the utensils." Clyde stopped her. "Open the basement door for me. We're not eating the ice cream for a while anyway."

Susie demurred. Obviously Clyde wanted every moment spent with her that he could capture. She was pleased. Clyde was a goot catch as a husband, but Amos Troyer was better. Wilma had been right on that point.

"Ready!" Clyde poured some of the saltwater onto the concrete floor, then gripped the ice cream maker with both hands.

Susie saw his biceps rippling and looked away. If Clyde noticed her admiring his muscles, she would be mortified. She owed him for the evening at the school auction, but the $600 the man had paid for the sticky buns would carry him only so far.

Clyde heaved the ice cream maker aloft, and Susie rushed forward to open the basement door. She followed him up the stairs and into the starlit night. He didn't slow his pace as they moved across the yard. He had left most of the ice and salt in the mixer. The ice cream inside the metal canister wouldn't melt before they were ready to eat, but the weight he carried was tremendous.

Susie hurried ahead of him to hold open the barn door. The soft glow of the lanterns fell on his face, and she gave him a warm smile.

He had helped with the ice cream making when he could have spent his time doing something else, and that was worth a smile or two.

He set the ice cream freezer down in the center of the barn floor with a loud thump. Several of the girls gave him admiring gazes, but he ignored them.

"You are sitting with me," he told Susie. Clearly he wouldn't take no for an answer.

She settled on a chair beside him as the young people's chatter again filled the barn.

He pulled a heap of green corn ears closer and handed one to her. "Hope there are no worms," he said with a grin.

Susie laughed along with him. She was not afraid of the worms that sometimes burrowed into the sweet corn before harvest. She was a farm girl, used to the natural things of life. Clyde had to know this.

His wink said he did. "So did you bring cinnamon rolls and doughnuts especially for me?"

"You can have all you want."

His smile faltered. "I had hoped after the school auction that there would be something special between us."

"There is," she told him. "We are friends."

His face fell. "You know what I mean. Can I take you home this Sunday evening for a date?"

Her head spun.

"Please," he whispered.

"You'll have to wait for my answer," she finally choked out.

"That means no, right?"

"We shouldn't talk about this here." She forced a smile. "What were you doing today on the farm?"

"Just the usual." His disappointment showed, and he lapsed into silence.

Her gaze drifted around the lantern-lit room. Amos was seated across the barn floor chatting with several of the young men. At least he wasn't with Charity who had a large pile of green corn ears at her feet. The girl would never finish that much by herself, but Charity obviously didn't know this. She was working diligently with her head down. None of the community men around Charity made any attempt at conversation.

"What are you thinking?" Clyde murmured.

Heat raced up her neck. She was not about to repeat her thoughts on Charity.

"You're not reconsidering, are you?"

"I can't let you take me home on a date right now. Sorry."

He lowered his head and busied himself with the cornhusking.

Charity tackled the pile of green corn ears in front of her with a vengeance. In the mood she was in, she shouldn't have left her apartment tonight, but things must be faced. She could not go through the rest of her life avoiding situations that made her long for David. Back when they had been together, he would be seated close beside her at this moment. He would know how many ears of corn to gather at their feet. He would know because he knew such things, plus a thousand more.

Paint responded to her touch on the canvas in a language she couldn't express any other way. He had supplied what she lacked. He had filled the voids she missed. He had known she couldn't bake, and he had loved her in spite of her deficiencies.

Charity winced. What Amish woman didn't know how to bake? But there she was, completely clueless about how to create the delicacies that Wilma and Susie produced. They were attended tonight by men who glowed at every smile the girls deemed fit to send their way. No man was by Charity's side, but she didn't want just any man. She wanted David. She would never open her heart again. She couldn't—and yet she had to. She couldn't go on living like this.

She didn't dare wipe her eyes. What Amish girl cried at a cornhusking? These were happy occasions when the community's young people gathered to enjoy each other's company and make memories that would last a lifetime. Could she ever become part of this community?

As she ripped the green husk from an ear, a hideous white grub lifted its head as if to reach for her, the rest of its fat body hidden in the yellow kernels. She screamed and threw the ear of corn.

Silence gripped the barn, filled only with the hiss of the gas lanterns hung from the beams.

She covered her face with both hands. Now she would die from shame. Should she go home? Make a dash outside? But how was she to find her horse? Grandpa Byler was not here, and in her shame she wasn't sure she'd be able to locate the barn door.

A hand lightly touched her arm. "Are you okay?"

Charity peeked out between her fingers. James Troyer's concerned face was inches away.

"It was just a worm." He held up the offending ear of corn, empty of its host. "But those can be an awful shock. I almost passed out myself when I saw my first one."

"You did not," she said.

"Well, maybe not," he allowed with a grin. "But you'll be okay. Can I sit with you?"

She couldn't refuse him, not with the whole room watching.

He sat down as if he had drawn the same conclusion, but at least everyone stopped staring at them.

"Thanks for sitting with me."

"My pleasure." He still appeared concerned. "So you are the community's new schoolteacher. Are you missing Holmes County?"

Charity took a deep breath. "Yah, but it's nice out here."

"I saw your painting at Wilma and Susie's bakery. Quite excellent, if you ask me. Are you the same CLM whose paintings were once in a little shop near Berlin, Ohio? My brother and I loved the one of the waterfalls."

Her head felt light, as if it would float away. Charity nodded, unable to speak.

"Amazing! What does the *L* stand for?"

Heat rose into her face.

"Ah, the mysterious painter with an equally mysterious middle name. But you can surely tell me."

"Lynn," she whispered. "Charity Lynn Martin.

"There," he said with a smile. "That wasn't so hard, was it?"

And together they tackled the pile of corn at her feet.

6

A week later, Wilma opened the bakery door and stepped inside. She lit the lantern, and with a soft *poof,* light flooded the bakery. She stepped back to yawn. Four o'clock was too early to awaken from a sound sleep, but Friday was a busy day, and there was a volleyball game planned for the young people tonight.

This was another chance to impress the Troyer brothers. She and Susie should take along a special baked item to undo the attention Charity had stolen from James at Grandpa's cornhusking party. But certainly it wouldn't happen again, and there was an upside to Charity's meltdown. Her reputation had suffered greatly. It would have crashed even more if James hadn't chatted with her for the rest of the evening. He had not left the schoolteacher's side until her buggy was hitched up and headed down the road.

What was wrong with him? Didn't he have the sense to leave Charity alone? Maybe he was just kind. But what if that wasn't what had kept him beside her all evening?

Wilma glared at the far wall where the stallion painting was draped in shadows. She should ask Grandpa to remove the painting. But how could she explain the request? He had a soft heart for the teacher. James, on the other hand, had no vested interest in the woman. Or he shouldn't, anyway.

Wilma sighed as the door opened and Susie slipped inside.

"We should bake something special today," Wilma announced.

Susie rubbed her eyes. "Everything is selling well. Why change?"

"I mean for the volleyball game tonight. Apparently common cinnamon rolls and doughnuts don't get the Troyer brothers' full attention."

A smile flickered on Susie's face. "What would you have done if the worm had been in your ear of corn? Clyde said it was a fat one."

"Don't tease me. It's not funny. I'd almost give the girl credit for picking a wormy ear on purpose, but who would do that?" She shuddered. "Charity should go back where she came from instead of stealing our men."

"The Troyers just arrived in the community. Can we really call them ours?"

"Whose side are you on?"

Susie shrugged. "I feel sorry for Charity. Too bad Clyde didn't go over and comfort her. I'm sure he thought of it, but he didn't dare offend me, and I didn't want to offend him by encouraging him to do it."

Wilma groaned. "How come things always go the wrong way for me? You should have pushed him."

Susie laughed. "It is a tangled mess." She opened a large bowl of flour and measured out a scoop. "But I didn't get out of bed at this hour to discuss Charity."

"The girl doesn't get up at four to paint. That's how unfair things are."

"Maybe I should just forget about Amos," Susie suggested. "Clyde is quite interested in me."

"Don't you consider settling for less. Amos is a much better catch, and you know it."

Susie nodded. "That he is."

Wilma put on her apron. "We can do this. I found the right recipe last evening for cinnamon-raisin Danish swirls. We can serve them this evening after the game."

Susie made a face. "There will be no homemade ice cream at a volleyball game unless I miss my guess."

"All the more chance for our swirls to shine."

"Or flop."

Ignoring her cousin, Wilma found the recipe in the far drawer. Discouragement was easy at four o'clock in the morning. In the end, they would snag the Troyer brothers as their husbands. Wilma glared at the stallion on the wall again. Charity would not stop them. Wilma and Susie would both become Troyers and have happy grandchildren gathered around them in their old age. They would retell this story a thousand times on the front porch swing. James and Amos would deny the role that baking had played in the conquest, but the truth would be told.

Wilma laid out the recipe and gathered the ingredients for the dough. This was the important step for cinnamon rolls and sticky buns, so the same should be true for fancy cinnamon-raisin Danish swirls. Dough was the foundation on which everything lay. She could handle this. Only a small corner of the baking counter was needed for the extra project, so nothing would be lost. There was still plenty of space for their daily supply of other baked goods.

She hummed a happy tune while she worked.

"What is that song?" Susie finally asked.

Wilma's face reddened. "An English tune I heard at the grocery store while I was in town several weeks ago."

"Do you know the words?"

Wilma shook her head. "I couldn't sing them anyway."

"Charity probably can."

"Did you have to say that?" Wilma exploded. "I need the courage to make these Danish swirls."

"Singing doesn't do much goot in keeping house." Susie pressed down on the cinnamon bread dough with a roller pin.

"See, then we have nothing to worry about."

But obviously they did. Susie's face said the same thing as they continued to work, but they mustn't despair. The old-fashioned ways of the community would prevail. The wisdom of the ages could not be wrong. Painting and fancy singing were influenced by the English world, a world that lay far outside the boundaries of the community. That Charity sought to blur the lines was reason enough for any Amish man to reject her.

"There!" Wilma added the last bit of flour to the dry ingredients and stirred vigorously. "Don't look so disheartened, Susie. No man will be able to resist these."

Susie frowned but said nothing.

A long line of buggies was already parked in the barnyard when Susie drove into Deacon Jonas's lane with Wilma seated on the buggy seat beside her.

"Don't come to a sudden stop," Wilma warned. "Our Danish swirls might slide."

"Whoa," Susie called to the family horse, Midnight. The animal lumbered to a slow halt.

"He's coming," Wilma said in a hushed tone.

Susie didn't ask who. Wilma would only use that tone for one man.

"The Danish swirls are already working," Wilma whispered.

Susie let go of the reins as Wilma lowered herself gracefully down to the buggy step, then the ground. "Goot evening, James."

James's deep chuckle hung in the evening air. "And a goot evening to you, Wilma and Susie."

"Goot evening." Susie climbed down.

"Thank you so much for coming to help us unhitch," Wilma chirped. "That is what you came for, is it not?"

"Of course." James began to unfasten the tug on his side and sent a smile across the shafts to Susie. "How are you this evening?"

"Just fine."

Wilma had disappeared behind the buggy. Was her cousin about to produce her Danish swirls with a flourish and swing them under James's nose?

"Do you two always travel together?" James came around to stand at Midnight's head.

"Most of the time. I'm an only child, and Wilma's siblings are younger."

"I see." He rested his hand on Midnight's halter. "Shall I take him to the barn?"

"If you want to. Just let us know where he is so I can find him later."

He shook his finger at her. "Now listen. I will help you girls hitch up after the game. So don't fuss or go to find your horse." He grinned.

Wilma came out from behind the buggy on her tiptoes, with a plate of Danish swirls in each hand.

Susie placed herself between her cousin and James. "That's so kind of you. Thanks."

He peered around Susie and let go of Midnight's bridle to step closer. "What would these morsels be called? Heavenly delights perhaps?"

Wilma's laugh was throaty. "Just Danish swirls, the recipe fresh from the old country." She held out the plates to him. "I found the recipe in our cookbook this week."

His face glowed as he eyed the treats. "Do I have to wait? How about one right now? They look so delicious."

Wilma pulled the Danish swirls back. "You'll have to wait, but I'll make sure there are two of them waiting especially for you."

"Ah . . ." He drew a long breath over the baked goodies. "Absolutely unbelievable."

Susie joined in their laughter as Midnight turned his head to stare at them. The horse appeared to wonder what was going on. Susie stroked Midnight's head. They were acting foolishly, but Wilma's methods seemed to be working. How could she complain?

"I'll see you girls later." James took Midnight from her and led the horse toward the barn.

Wilma raised an eyebrow at Susie. "How's that for success?"

"You are overdoing it." Susie nudged Wilma. "Let's not stand here staring after the man."

Wilma swung into motion, and the Danish swirls almost went flying. Susie snatched one of the plates from her distracted cousin's hand.

"We got the man's attention," Wilma declared, as if that justified everything.

Susie didn't answer as they glided up the sidewalk to the front door.

"What have you there, Wilma?" a man called out from one of the buggies that was heading up the lane.

"Can I have some?" another asked.

Wilma ignored them and continued onward.

Deacon Jonas's Frau, Ann, met them at the front door with a big smile. "Goot evening, Wilma and Susie. You brought something! I was hoping you would. The men get hungry after a game."

"Danish swirls," Wilma gushed. "Freshly baked this morning."

Ann took a peek and seemed suitably impressed. "You girls have quite the reputation in the community. Neither of you should have any problem getting the husband of your choice. Any decisions yet?"

"That takes some time, you know," Wilma deadpanned. "We have to pray about who the man should be."

Ann beamed. "I'm glad to hear that you are making this a serious matter. Choosing a life partner is a very important decision."

"That it is."

Susie met Ann's gaze. "Wilma is praying—*and* baking."

Ann hid her amusement with a quick flourish of her apron. "Sometimes that is part of the journey and an equally important one."

Wilma didn't comment, but rushed into the kitchen with her Danish swirls.

Susie hung back to join a small gathering of girls by the front door. She greeted them with a nod and a smile. The volleyball game would begin in a moment, and they probably hoped, as she did, that a man would ask them to play beside him. Amos might do that for her if he had the intent and the nerve. She hadn't seen Clyde yet, but he would maneuver for the opportunity if Amos didn't. Wilma was likely to throw their Danish swirls out of Ann's kitchen window if James didn't give her a special place by his side at the game.

Charity slipped into her apartment a little after ten and searched for a match in the darkness. She stubbed her bare toe against the desk leg, then lowered herself to the hardwood floor to rub her foot with both hands. The pain reached up her back and into her neck.

The tears came quickly. This was more punishment on top of the evening's humiliation. How much more could she take? Would the memory of David never die? He was miles away, back in Holmes County, likely in the arms of another girl. Charity pressed her thumb into her foot and let grief wash over her.

Long moments passed before the ache subsided and her sobs

ceased. She was an intruder. She should never have come to Nebraska. What had possessed her to believe she could make a fresh start? That journey must involve certain aspects she hadn't anticipated: another life, another community, another love. Her heart didn't want that. This community didn't want that. Everyone had a place, except her.

She had played alone at the volleyball game, stuck between two random couples who spent the evening with their attention on each other instead of the game. On the other side of the court Wilma and Susie had played host to the Troyer brothers. All Charity's stamina had been needed to make it through the hours until she could leave.

Her heart could not love again. She would never make a proper Amish housewife. She could barely make a cake mix taste right, let alone prepare Danish swirls like the ones Wilma and Susie had brought to the game.

If she didn't stop thinking, she was going to go mad. She told herself to just breathe.

Charity let go of her foot and pulled herself upright. She found the match in the drawer and lit the kerosene lamp. By the flickering flames of the lamp she lifted the cloth from the painting. She was too tired to work tonight, but the partially finished scene flowed out before her until she could see the whole picture. The shepherd had his arms protectively around his lambs, his gaze directed toward the distant waters where the trees, the grass, and the abundance lay.

"He cares," she whispered.

7

Wilma swiped the crumbs from the counter into the small wastebasket. She stepped back to survey the floor. It would need a thorough sweeping before they were ready for their first customers. Monday was a slow sale day, but Susie had wanted their usual quota baked. Two of Deacon Jonas's children had taken ill over the weekend, and the family could use the items they didn't sell. With Ann's household of hungry Kinner to feed, their contribution would be greatly appreciated.

Wilma grabbed the broom from the front closet and briskly swept the foyer, scooping up the small pile of debris before she moved on.

She ought to dance with joy this morning. James had given her a sweet smile at the church services yesterday, right after Grandpa Byler had completed his sermon. James seemed impressed with her and with the community, which was crucial to her plans. She could tell that he liked the preaching, the fellowship, the young folks. The volleyball game had been a smashing success last week. Even Susie had admitted that great progress had been made with the Troyer brothers. Wilma was sure James would ask her home for a date soon—maybe even this weekend. She could see him in her mind's eye, bursting through the bakery door to declare his love for her.

Wilma closed her eyes, imagining the scene. James would have a happy glow on his face. He would be thinking of their future life together, knowing that he would never lack in goot cooking. There would always be food on their kitchen table. Their cupboard would never be bare. Even in illness she would do her part, and if she couldn't, Susie would be nearby to help. They would be together as they had always been, supporting each other and caring for each other's needs.

That was what life in the community supplied, and James knew that she played her part well. Why else would he have spent the whole game playing by her side while Amos did the same with Susie? The door of opportunity had opened, and the Lord had blessed. There was no other conclusion on the matter.

"Coffee's ready," Susie called from the back room.

"Be right there." Wilma swatted at a spiderweb under the counter before gathering up the last of the debris and emptying the dustpan in the wastebasket.

"I made it strong," Susie said as Wilma joined her.

Wilma did a little jig before she settled into a chair.

"I don't think you need coffee." Susie chuckled.

"Aren't you happy? Amos did give you a smile or two yesterday at church, didn't he?"

"He did," Susie admitted. "But he also smiled at Charity. I even saw them talking together after lunch had been served."

Wilma froze. "Why didn't you tell me earlier?"

"There hasn't been a chance, but they have a right to talk about whatever they wish. I am not Amos's Frau."

Wilma took a deep breath. "There is probably a sensible reason. Likely one of the younger Troyer siblings is having trouble in school."

"Charity would speak with Ezra or Lydia about that."

"Don't take me literally," Wilma scolded. "I'm just saying that there is probably a perfectly logical explanation. After the volleyball game Friday evening, we have nothing to worry about."

"Amos was sweet to me that evening." Susie smiled.

Wilma filled a cup with coffee. "I guess I do need this after all."

Susie's smile vanished. "Sorry for saying something."

Wilma shrugged. "There are always bumps in the road. We must keep up our hopes."

"Do you think I actually could be a proper Frau for someone like Amos?"

"Don't doubt yourself. Our Danish swirls sealed our reputation with the Troyer brothers. Not that anyone else needed convincing, but they are newcomers to the community and had a right to their doubts."

The front door opened.

Wilma sat bolt upright. "Is that Grandpa?"

"I'll go see." Susie set down her coffee cup.

Wilma waited. She should stand and greet Grandpa, but talk of Charity and the Troyers had left her mentally exhausted.

Soft voices murmured behind her. That was not Grandpa's chuckle. The Troyer brothers were here! Hadn't she imagined James stopping by only minutes ago? She had been caught sleeping at her post.

She jumped to her feet, sending her coffee cup flying. Streams of dark brew ran over the tabletop. Wilma yanked off her apron and sponged the liquid. She pressed the wrinkles out of her dress. Then she panicked. Her spare apron was in the front closet. Susie was wearing an apron, so if Wilma walked out without one, James and Amos would think she had been slacking in her morning labors. Excuses would only make things worse.

Wilma willed the pounding of her heart to slow. It was all right. They had coffee and plenty of baked goods to offer the brothers. Men forgot a lot when they were eating wunderbah food.

"Wilma," Susie called. "James and Amos have stopped by."

Now they would think she didn't want to meet them, but her feet were frozen in fear.

The Troyer brothers had asked to play by their sides on Friday evening, and now they had stopped in for a Monday morning visit. Susie admitted that Wilma had been correct in her evaluation. Would Amos soon ask Susie home on a date? Perhaps even before the two left this morning?

"We're not disturbing you, are we?" James asked.

"Of course not." Susie waved her hand at the back room. "We have coffee and these baked items ready. You are welcome to stay."

"Just the words I wanted to hear," James said with a big grin.

Susie glanced over her shoulder. Where was Wilma? She must have heard Susie call.

"You wouldn't have any more of those Danish swirls around, would you?" Amos asked, followed by a deep chuckle. "Sorry. I just had to ask."

Susie forced a laugh. "I'm afraid not."

Wilma burst out of the back room as if shot from a cannon. She wasn't wearing her apron.

Both of the brothers whirled around to stare at her.

"Goot morning," Wilma almost shouted. Her face was red and beaded with sweat.

"I see you've been hard at work." James appeared concerned. "Sorry to intrude, but we thought we'd take the chance."

"This is perfect," Wilma gushed. "We have coffee ready and our baked items for the day."

"What will this cost us?" Amos asked.

"Thousands," Wilma retorted with a grin.

Everyone laughed.

"I will get the coffee," Susie said. "Both of you want sugar and cream?"

"That's right," they said together.

"Plenty of sugar," Amos added.

Susie gave him a sweet smile and hurried into the back room. She didn't have the comebacks that Wilma did, but Amos seemed to appreciate her efforts to serve him. Susie's heart pounded as she prepared the coffee cups and grabbed two plates. She noticed a faint brown stain spread over the center of the table. Wilma had spilled her coffee. So that's why she'd taken so long. At least she had not invited the two back here for coffee and sweets. Susie grabbed a washcloth, ran it under the water, and wiped the tabletop clean.

"We made plenty of baked goods for a Monday morning," Wilma was saying when Susie returned to the front with a tray. "If there are any left, we'll take them down to Deacon Jonas's place this evening. So help yourself to whatever you want."

"Why don't we get baked items delivered to our doorstep every evening?" James joked.

"Only sick people get that." Wilma shook her finger at him.

"Then I will see if I can conjure up a high fever tomorrow."

Laughter filled the small bakery.

Susie slid the tray onto the counter and handed the brothers their plates and cups of coffee. "Hope you enjoy."

Both brothers cut sizable portions of cinnamon rolls and ate while they sipped from their cups.

"Perfect," they declared together.

James gazed up at Charity's painting on the wall. "How much better can life get? We are at a bakery where they give out free baked goods, and the place is run by two lovely girls who have a beautiful painting on their wall. Charity must be happy to have her painting displayed here in such splendor."

"I'm sure she is," Wilma said with an edge in her voice.

James tilted his head. "Why did you say the painting was here? It must be worth a lot of money. The one we saw in Ohio cost over $1,000."

"So that means we're prosperous." Wilma laughed. "That's why we can give out free baked goods."

James chuckled. "What is the story behind your grandfather's acquisition of the painting?"

Susie stepped forward. "Grandpa made the purchase at this year's school auction and decided to hang the painting here."

"The auction. That explains how your grandfather was willing to pay the high price."

Should she tell the truth about what Grandpa had paid for the painting?

"Do either of you want another cinnamon roll?" Wilma asked.

James and Amos didn't answer as they studied the painting.

"It's not often that you meet an Amish girl who can paint at that level," Amos said. "I wonder where Charity learned."

"The girl has talent," James added.

"More cinnamon rolls?" Wilma asked again. "Sorry we didn't think to make Danish swirls this morning."

James smiled at her. "You can't have everything all the time."

"We'll take some cinnamon rolls to go for our lunch, if you don't object," Amos said.

"Of course not!" Wilma exclaimed. "We should have thought of that."

Susie darted into the back room and returned with two plastic bags.

Wilma slid the cinnamon rolls inside. "There." She handed the bags over with a smile.

"Thank you so much," James said.

"We'll have to do this more often." Amos put on his hat and tipped the rim.

Wilma followed them to the door, fluttering about. They left with a wave and a shout from Wilma . . . "Come as often as you want!"

Susie found a stool and sat down. Something had gone horribly wrong. But what?

Wilma joined her. "If only I had my extra apron in the back room, this would not have happened." She pointed at Charity's painting. "You awful, wicked thing. You are to blame for this, but you will not win! You will not!"

"They liked our cinnamon rolls," Susie reminded her cousin. "And they did stop by."

Wilma whirled around. "There is nothing positive about this morning. James and Amos stood in *our* bakery admiring *Charity's* painting!" Her voice rose to a wail. "The old ways are right. I know they are. Homemaking, cooking, baking, Kinner—that's what the men of the community want. We will not give up."

"We really should get ready for the day," Susie told her. "The first customers will be arriving soon."

"My apron!" Wilma exclaimed. "I haven't put on my spare apron."

"What happened to the one you had?" Susie asked.

Wilma didn't answer. Instead, she dashed to the front closet, opened the door, and buried her face in a fresh, white apron.

With her work finished and dusk falling, Charity walked to the front window of her apartment. There wouldn't be much of a sunset tonight. There were too many clouds on the horizon, thick masses of thunderheads that threatened rain through the night. She should work on the painting this evening, but there were too many clouds over her heart. Her teaching was the only thing that lifted her spirits: the laughter of her students, their love for her, and their simple thanks for her efforts.

A movement caught her eye. A buggy was coming. But who? One of the student's parents perhaps, coming with a reprimand for how she taught school? What other explanation was there for a late-evening visit?

She stepped back from the window as the buggy slowed and pulled into her driveway. She couldn't take more pain. Not tonight.

Charity trembled when the buggy stopped. She wanted to run away, but she couldn't. This must also be faced somehow.

Amos Troyer emerged from the buggy. Then his brother James came around the other side. They tied their horse to the hitching post and headed for the front door.

Charity forced herself to move and to breathe. There was some logical explanation for this visit. But what? She opened the door before they knocked. "Goot evening. What a surprise."

"We're on our way home." James grinned sheepishly. "We thought we'd stop by and take a peek at this painting of yours our sister keeps talking about. That is, if you don't mind our dirty work clothing."

"Of course not." Charity clung to the doorframe. "But it's just a painting and still unfinished."

"We have long admired your work—unbeknownst to us." Amos chuckled. "My brother told you we saw one of your paintings in Ohio."

"And the stallion at the bakery," James added. "That is truly a work of art. We would be honored if we could have a peek at your current work."

"Well, yah, I guess." Charity moved away from the door. "Please come in."

Amos brushed off his pant legs. "I imagine a teacher has her house spotless."

"I wish," Charity choked out. "But the painting really isn't worth the fuss."

"We'll be the judges of that." James grinned.

Charity led the way to the cloth-draped painting. She was going to pass out any moment. "You can take a peek." She barely waved her hand. She felt too weak to remove the covering.

James reverently lifted the cloth, and the two gazed at the partially finished painting for a long time. Just when she thought she would scream with the suspense, James murmured, "True talent. Who taught you?"

Charity's head swam. How could he think this was talent? Her paintings had brought nothing but sorrow to her life.

"You don't have to tell us if you don't want to," Amos added, replacing the covering.

Charity spoke slowly. "There is a small craft shop back in Holmes County. They offered lessons and even had a teacher up from Ohio State University for summer classes. I went, and I guess that's where I learned." She hung her head.

"Thanks for showing us the piece," James said. "It is truly priceless."

"You don't have to thank me." The words dried up in Charity's mouth. "But that is kind of you to say."

James gave her a warm smile. "We should be going, but perhaps we can see the painting again when you are finished?"

Charity nodded and ushered them to the door.

"Goot night," they told her.

She forced herself to stay outside until they had climbed into their buggy. They waved on their way out of the driveway.

Charity closed the door behind her and slowly sank to the floor.

8

With Thanksgiving Day fast approaching, no youth gatherings were scheduled for the near future. The time was filled with preparations for family events. There were houses to clean and extra beds that must be aired out before the arrival of visiting relatives.

"Be sure and close the bakery early today," Mamm had reminded Wilma before she left well before dawn. "I need your help."

"We'll close by three," Wilma had promised.

Susie had a similar message when she stepped inside the bakery door. "Mamm said I have to help at the house this afternoon."

Wilma nodded. "So did mine. I promised to close by three, so how much shall we bake this morning?"

"I don't think we should cut back too much," Susie decided without hesitation. "Deacon Jonas's Frau is ill now. We can give them what we have left."

"That would be appreciated." Wilma wanted to suggest another stop, but didn't. The Troyer brothers were a sore subject at the moment. Apparently they were having trouble deciding between proper Amish women and flighty painters.

"You're not thinking what I'm thinking, are you?" Susie asked.

"Yah, but I won't."

"We've pushed the issue far enough."

"There was no damage done."

"Really! James and Amos stopped by Charity's for a peek at the new painting, the very day they were here. They were quite impressed, I was told."

Wilma leaned against the counter. "Are you sure?"

"I heard Amos talking about their visit with Elmer Yutsy, but the children should also know. Ask Miriam if you don't believe me." Susie busied herself at the flour bin.

"Confound it," Wilma muttered. "Why did they see me without my apron? That was to blame for this whole thing."

Susie slowly measured out the flour. "I think you are overreacting."

"Someday I will take that painting down and throw it out the window."

"Grandpa put it there," Susie reminded her before she added another scoop of flour.

Wilma banged her hand on the counter. "I know what we can do. Let's close. We have been working hard enough, and our families could use our help for the entire day. I'll go up to your house this morning, and you can help me this afternoon."

Susie's eyes grew large.

"We deserve the break," Wilma insisted. "And the first of the week is slow anyway."

"Why don't we bake this morning and ask Grandpa and Grandma to watch the shop for us when we finish?"

Wilma hesitated a moment. "I guess that would be an idea."

"I'll go ask right now." Susie dashed out the door and returned ten minutes later. "Grandpa said they would be happy to sell out everything we bake this morning."

Wilma grunted. "Were they up?"

"Grandpa was reading in his rocker, and Grandma was fixing breakfast."

Wilma smiled. Something was still right in the world. She must not doubt that, even in the storms of life.

They worked quickly, and the first batch of cinnamon rolls was finished before the blush of dawn crept into the eastern sky.

"I'm fixing coffee," Wilma told Susie. "Grandpa won't be here for an hour yet."

But the hinges squeaked on the front door before the coffeepot was full, and Grandpa entered.

Wilma stuck her head out of the back room. "Thanks for taking care of this for us."

"Can't keep the womenfolk away from their housecleaning," Grandpa grumbled. "Your grandma has been turning the house upside down since last week."

Wilma gave him a warm smile. "Who is coming for Thanksgiving Day?"

"That's the point." Grandpa lowered himself into a chair by the counter and scowled. "We're going to your family's place."

Wilma laughed. "The cleaning must be done regardless. I'm a woman. I know."

"I suppose so," Grandpa allowed. "How are things going with the bakery? I haven't paid much attention beyond keeping the checkbook balanced."

"Is there still money left?" Susie asked in a worried tone.

Grandpa grinned. "You girls are doing so well. Much better than your grandmother and I did. You must have the whole English community stopping by for doughnuts and rolls."

Wilma smiled at Grandpa. "Do you want coffee?"

"I'd take a cup, but you still haven't told me how you are doing, slaving away at this place."

Wilma lifted her head high. "Like you said, the community favors our products, and hard work is goot for anyone."

"You girls are keeping long hours. Sometimes it can get a bit much."

Wilma patted him on the arm. "We can handle it. Can't we, Susie?"

Susie nodded. "We were raised to work hard."

Grandpa appeared to relax. "I wouldn't expect anything less from my granddaughters. Now if the two of you could learn how to paint, your lives would be well-rounded."

"Grandpa!" Wilma bit back the rest of her sharp retort, then dashed into the back room.

From the look on his face, Grandpa wasn't fooled when she came back with cups of coffee. "What is going on, Wilma? I was only teasing."

"I know, but it hurt."

"The Troyer brothers stopped by the other morning and were admiring the painting." Susie took it upon herself to inform Grandpa.

"I see." Grandpa shifted on his seat. "I'm not surprised that my granddaughters would set their bonnets for such handsome young men, but surely you don't object to men who admire beautiful art."

"Charity is stealing their hearts," Wilma wailed. "The woman is awful."

Grandpa clucked his tongue. "You must be imagining things. Charity had her troubles back in Holmes County. Maybe I should tell you about some of them so you don't worry."

"She did?" Susie asked.

"We're not talking about Charity's troubles," Wilma cut in. "The woman is after our men."

Grandpa stroked his beard. "The Troyer brothers seem quite impressed with the two of you, and there's nothing wrong with appreciating someone else's talent."

"I thought you would be on my side," Wilma huffed.

"I didn't know there were sides," Grandpa said gently. "I had hoped that Charity would fit well into the community."

"She has no right to our young men." Wilma whirled around to face him. "If Charity is so talented, why didn't she secure a boyfriend in Holmes County? There are plenty of men there—unlike Nebraska!"

"Come now," Grandpa chided. "You can have any man you want,

including James Troyer. Charity's story is a sad one, which I might tell you someday. But in the meantime, your attitude is not right. That will do you more harm than anything else."

"My reaction is perfectly understandable. Ask Susie if you don't believe me."

"I'm staying out of this," Susie said.

Grandpa twisted in his chair. "You have no interest in the Troyer brothers?"

Susie colored quickly.

"See, there's your answer." Wilma waved her hand in the air. "It's not fair that we have to deal with Charity at this crucial moment in our lives. A few years in the future, with our wedding vows said, I wouldn't care."

Grandpa smiled. "Both of you will do fine, regardless of how this goes. You have your baking skills, and you are great catches. Don't Abner and Clyde think so?"

"Abner!" Wilma flung her hands in the air. "Perhaps if James hadn't arrived, I'd agree. But I'm not settling for Abner now."

"I see." Grandpa gave them a sober expression. "I really don't think Charity will be a problem. She has a troubled road to travel, but it doesn't have to conflict with yours or Susie's."

"I think you're right." Wilma took a long sip of her coffee. "Sorry. I'll try to calm myself."

"Now that we have that settled, is there any chance you two could stop in at my place this morning and finish the cleaning for your grandmother?" Grandpa begged. "You could bring much peace to my weary soul."

Wilma fought a smile. "Anything for you, Grandpa."

"And for my part, I'll drop a hint in the Troyer brothers' ears about my capable and lovely granddaughters."

"They are here now," Susie gasped.

Wilma sprang to her feet.

"Well, well." Grandpa chuckled. "What do you know?"

Susie waited beside Grandpa while Wilma rushed to the door. "Goot morning!"

"She likes us," James quipped.

Strokes of heat raced up Susie's neck. Wilma was making a scene.

Amos grinned at Susie. "Don't worry. We're paying for the baked goodies this morning."

"But you don't have to. The thought never crossed my mind." Susie's face turned a blaze of red, but neither of the brothers appeared to notice as Wilma ushered them inside.

"The Troyer brothers!" Grandpa bellowed from his chair. "Goot to see you. Have my wunderbah granddaughters been treating their customers right?"

"No complaints," James said. "I'm afraid we have been nonpaying customers so far, but that is about to change. Mamm had her hands full yesterday with one of the younger children who was ill and stayed home from school. She told us to stop by and stock up on sticky buns and cinnamon rolls—enough for our lunch at least." He plunked down a bill on the countertop.

"Excellent," Grandpa said. "I was getting ready to enjoy a few myself."

"What are you doing up this time of the morning?" Amos asked.

"This old man doesn't sleep," Grandpa said. "I'm here to tend the store for my lovely granddaughters while they clean houses in preparation for our family's Thanksgiving dinner."

"Why have we no invitations to these dinners?" James teased.

"You both could come to my parents' place for Thanksgiving," Wilma offered, "along with the rest of your family."

Grandpa smiled. "Sounds like you're invited, boys."

"Of course Mamm and Daett have to agree," Amos told him.

"They will," James assured his brother. "So let us gather up our loot and take our leave. We don't want to keep these beautiful women from their work."

Grandpa waved his hand. "Sit down, boys. What's the rush? There are cinnamon rolls and coffee on the house. Surely you have the time to chat with an old man? Catch me up on how things are going now that you are settled in the community."

James laughed. "We're still settling in, but work has picked up this week. We didn't expect things to be easy starting up a new business."

"I can imagine." Grandpa waited while Susie set coffee cups in front of the brothers.

"Same as the other morning?" She gave them both a warm smile.

They nodded, wrapped up in their conversation with Grandpa.

"We went over to see Charity's new painting." James motioned to the stallion hanging on the wall. "The scene should be almost as goot as that one."

Wilma lifted her nose in the air but didn't comment.

"Charity has talent," Amos added.

"That she does," Grandpa agreed. "Charity had a lot of success selling her paintings in Ohio."

"She has formal training," Amos said. "Did you know that?"

James nudged his brother. "I don't think you were supposed to say that. Grandpa Byler is a bishop."

The men laughed.

"Charity is more than welcome in this community," Grandpa said. "She can pursue her painting with or without formal training."

Wilma ducked into the back room, which was just as well. James and Amos soon finished their coffee, paid for their cinnamon rolls, and left.

"Where's Wilma?" Grandpa asked.

Susie shook her head.

Grandpa solemnly stroked his beard. "That girl has nothing to worry about."

It was goot of Grandpa to say, but from the conversation she had just heard, Wilma had plenty to worry about. James Troyer especially was deeply impressed with Charity *and* her paintings.

That evening, with the gas lantern hung on the ceiling above her, Charity touched the paintbrush to the canvas. Unchecked papers were piled on her desk at the schoolhouse, but urgency gripped her. She wanted to capture the vision that danced in front of her eyes before the colors faded.

Charity glanced at the clock. Eight o'clock and she hadn't eaten since lunch. She stepped back and studied the outlines of the forms. The distant oasis lay ahead of the flock of sheep. The look on the shepherd's face was one of concern but also of confidence. His sheep would be safe, contentedly grazing on lush grass.

Charity moved farther back. No obvious problems revealed themselves. Maybe by the light of day a few touch-ups would be needed, but nothing serious. She had painted again in the midst of her uncertainty, and again it had soothed her. Would peace find her and perhaps love? Was this community a new beginning?

The Troyer brothers were obviously taken with her paintings. Was James interested in her personally? Should she even consider his attentions? Did she dare? David's love was so fresh on her heart, the wound so open. Perhaps this was the healing, a man who could walk by her side without the condemnation of the community thundering down on their heads.

Could she open her heart? Could she forget David? Perhaps if she could return James's kind smiles, love might grow again. The least she could do was give the man a chance.

Charity rubbed her temples and set down her brush. There was paperwork waiting at the schoolhouse, and she was starving. Slowly, she walked to the icebox as exhaustion swept over her.

9

Around midmorning on Thanksgiving, Wilma transferred the last of the cinnamon roll pans to the highest cupboard shelf and stood back to shake her white apron vigorously.

Nearby, Miriam sneezed.

Wilma frowned at her younger sister. "I know I didn't shake off that many crumbs."

"You're all in a huff and worried about James Troyer. You've done nothing this morning but work on your cinnamon rolls."

"How do you know about James?"

"The whole community knows that you're chasing him."

Wilma gave her apron another sharp shake. "It's not a chase—it's a catch. If you pay attention to your cooking and housekeeping duties, you might get the chance to snag a wunderbah husband like James yourself someday."

Miriam smirked. "Does that include painting lessons? Becky told me James is quite taken with Teacher Charity's paintings."

"Don't get sassy with me. The community's old ways always win. Take these cinnamon rolls for example. For years to come, James will remember that he ate them at our place on Thanksgiving Day. Contrast that to paintings that hang on the wall and do nothing. What goot are they compared to something on the dinner table? You cannot eat a painting. They have no practical purpose."

Miriam appeared to process the point. "The Troyer brothers are new to the community. Maybe things are changing."

"Things are not changing," Wilma retorted, "and this conversation is beyond you. Isn't there work you should be doing? Susie and her Mamm are driving into the lane right now, and the Troyer family will arrive at any moment."

"So if things aren't changing, why did Grandpa hang Teacher Charity's painting in the bakery?"

Wilma hid the sharp intake of her breath with another vigorous shake of the apron. "Go let Susie and her Mamm in."

Miriam made a face at Wilma before she left.

The girl's words echoed in Wilma's mind. Why *had* Grandpa hung Charity's painting on the bakery wall? Wilma had assumed that Grandpa had done so because of his soft heart, but what if he had deeper reasons? Were things really changing in the community?

Wilma leaned on the edge of the counter. Nothing changed when it came to the old ways. She had to believe that. Kinner, housework, and goot food on the dinner table gave the community value.

Yet the last time James and Amos had visited the bakery, they had eaten their delicious cinnamon rolls and drunk the excellent coffee they had brewed. But they still had spoken of Charity's paintings with admiration. Did the Troyer brothers want baking and painting talents wrapped up in one woman? But that was impossible. Charity couldn't bake old-fashioned cinnamon rolls, and Wilma and Susie didn't waste time painting.

She chided herself for thinking these thoughts on this joyful day, with the opportunity to undo the damage and impress the brothers with their culinary skills.

Wilma opened the cupboard door to admire the warm cinnamon rolls on the top shelf. Their delicious aroma rolled out into the kitchen. She had outdone herself. Now if she could prepare the powdered sugar frosting with equal care, James would surely be won over today. There were no distracting paintings on the walls of the Wengerd home, just the scent of cinnamon rolls, along with turkey, cranberry sauce, fresh bread, corn, beans, and the pies they had made yesterday.

Wilma jumped when Susie walked in carrying a large pot. "You scared me."

Susie ignored the scolding, taking a deep breath. "I smelled them at the front door."

"I have to make the frosting yet."

"Are they in the cupboard?"

Wilma nodded.

Susie opened the door. "They look perfect, but didn't we already try cinnamon rolls?"

"I know, but there's nothing wrong with our cinnamon rolls. We must not lose our courage. I was extra careful to get the oven temperature right this morning and let the dough rise to the proper height. Our efforts will pay off if we don't lose heart."

"It might work." Susie stepped back from the counter. "My mouth is watering, and I see them almost every day."

"Thanks. I needed that."

Susie gave Wilma a soft smile. "I should have tried something special, but I was too weary after the mess the other morning."

Wilma sobered quickly. "Even I despaired, but this will be a great success today."

"What will be?" Mamm asked when she walked in with Susie's Mamm, Esther, in tow.

"The Thanksgiving meal," Wilma chirped, which was partially true. Winning James's heart and completing the food preparations had somehow become the same thing.

Esther set the plates of food she was carrying on the kitchen table. "I'm so surprised you have the Troyer family coming. They are new to the community. They must have had a dozen invitations for Thanksgiving dinner."

Wilma forced a smile. "James and Amos were at the bakery when Grandpa was there, and we invited them."

Esther clucked her tongue. "I must say you two have done well for yourselves with the bakery, and now you have two handsome men stopping by on their way to work."

"Don't count your chickens before they've hatched," Mamm warned.

"The Troyer brothers would be quite a catch, though," Esther concluded. "You have to admit that."

"Mamm," Susie protested, "we are both right here."

Esther smiled at her daughter. "Well, enough of that then. Let's get our things out on the table. Isn't that a buggy driving up the lane? Perhaps the Troyer family?"

There was silence for a moment while everyone listened. The clop of horse's hooves was unmistakable.

The two older women scurried into the living room to welcome the arriving family.

Wilma grabbed a bowl from the upper cabinet while Susie retrieved a bag of powdered sugar. They worked as a team, honed by their hours at the bakery until words were no longer needed. Susie measured the powdered sugar while Wilma heated the milk.

"I hope James asks you home today for a Sunday evening date," Susie whispered. "Wouldn't that be something?"

A thrill ran down Wilma's back. "I'm thinking he will."

The grandfather clock in the corner of the living room struck one.

Susie tried to breathe and smile at the same time. The table in front of her was laden with food. It was time for the guests to take their places.

"Don't be bashful." Wilma's Daett encouraged them, waving his hands about. "The food is only getting colder."

Grandpa and Grandma seated themselves, along with Ezra and Lydia Troyer. Their children should be next in line.

Susie jumped and stifled a gasp when Amos said directly behind her, "Can I have the honor of sitting beside you?" He grinned. "You already know that I don't bite."

"I-I . . . of course," Susie stammered.

"Allow me." Amos pulled out her chair. Not every young Amish man had such impeccable manners.

Blushing bright red, Susie sat down.

The others seated themselves around the table, with sly glances sent their way, and Grandpa led in giving thanks for the food.

Susie kept her head down after the "amen" was pronounced. Her face must have still blazed like the noonday sun.

Amos leaned over and asked quietly, "You all right?"

Just a little dizzy, Susie almost said, but how silly that would sound. Dizzy from what? She couldn't tell him how his presence affected her.

Amos's smile was kind. "You probably overexerted yourself in the kitchen."

"I'm okay. And women are supposed to work hard in the kitchen," she remarked, trying to steer the conversation to safer ground.

Amos chuckled as he passed the bowl of mashed potatoes.

Susie glanced around the table. Why wasn't James seated beside Wilma? In the kerfuffle of getting seated with Amos, she hadn't noticed before. Wilma deserved the first romantic overture from the Troyer brothers.

Amos held the meat plate for her, and she took a piece. "Enough?" He gave her the sweetest smile.

Susie nodded. Her voice would not work. She continued to wonder why James wasn't sitting with Wilma.

Next, Amos handed her a bowl of gravy.

As Susie reached for it, she nearly lost her grip. A mess of spilled gravy on the table was exactly what she didn't need. She forced herself to breathe evenly.

Across the table, Wilma was obviously trying to enjoy the meal, but a thundercloud had darkened her brow. James was at the other end of the table, chatting with Grandpa, who was seated across from him.

"Have you girls tried any new recipes at the bakery lately?" Amos asked. "Sorry we haven't had time to stop by, but with Thanksgiving coming, the construction hours have been from dawn to dusk."

"I can understand that." Susie accepted the bowl of corn he offered her and dished a large spoonful onto her plate. She caught Wilma's gaze. Sorrow pooled deeply in her cousin's eyes. Why had this happened after all the hard work Wilma had put into the meal?

"Have you tried any new recipes?" Amos repeated. "You can share your secrets with me."

Susie tried to focus on the conversation. "Nothing special, just the ordinary—cinnamon rolls and sticky buns."

"Nothing ordinary about them." Amos smacked his lips. "We are in for a treat today, with your baked goods on top of the excellent food we are already eating. Thanks again for the invitation."

"I'm sure you had plenty of them, being new in the community." The words slipped out before she could stop them.

His eyes twinkled. "We canceled the others to accept yours."

She stared at him. "You did not!"

"Three more invitations came in after yours. You just beat the crowd."

"I'm glad we did." Another rush of heat rose into her face. Amos would think her much too forward for a proper Amish housewife.

"So tell me more about the history of the community. Where did everyone come from?"

"From all over. My family is from Holmes County, way back when I was small."

He leaned over to her. "If Charity can make herself at home in the community with her paintings, I suppose we can."

Susie paled. What did he mean? "I hope everyone has been kind and open so far."

"Yes, you have a great community. I like it here. How old were you when your parents moved?"

Susie studied her food. She was embarrassing herself. If only Wilma didn't seem so haunted, she wouldn't be on edge.

"Didn't you want to move?" Amos appeared puzzled.

"Sorry, I was distracted for a moment. I was four or five. I've been here since I began attending school, and I love the community."

"Could you bake in the first grade?"

She caught his teasing tone. "You know that Amish girls learn to bake in their cribs."

Laughter crinkled his face. "I know my sisters did, but I mean your special touch with baking. Was it your grandfather's bakery that honed the skill?"

"I don't know."

"You are an only child, aren't you?"

"Is that a problem?" She glanced at him anxiously.

"No, but firstborns are often quite talented."

"Wilma is the talented one," Susie informed him. "I keep the books and help where I can."

"You underestimate yourself," Amos said. "I think you're plenty talented—as is Wilma, of course."

She ignored the comment. "Wilma made the cinnamon rolls by herself today."

He reached for the plate, which had begun its rounds. "So this is the special effort?"

"Wilma's trademark. That and the sticky buns."

He leaned out of his chair to call to his brother, "Wilma and Susie baked these cinnamon rolls."

"Of course they did! A day of thanksgiving indeed," James replied heartily.

"You shouldn't draw attention to us," Susie whispered.

Amos beamed at her. "You know James and I both love your baking."

Then why isn't James seated beside Wilma? she wanted to ask, but bit back the words.

He took a bite of his cinnamon roll and chewed it slowly. "Absolutely delicious," he pronounced.

"What are you two whispering about?" Wilma's Daett demanded.

"The cinnamon rolls," Amos answered. "They are unbelievable."

"They are," several voices chorused. "Who made them?"

"Wilma and Susie, naturally. They make the same delicious cinnamon rolls at their bakery!"

Susie stifled the instinct to correct. Wilma was smiling and acknowledging the praise, but the sadness was still in her eyes.

"I know that Wilma made these, but they taste the same." He leaned close again. "Can I take you home on Sunday evening for a date?"

Susie froze.

"Can I?" Amos appeared worried.

"Of course you can!" Susie blurted, then clamped both hands over her mouth.

He smiled and appeared quite pleased with himself.

When she looked across the table, she saw Wilma staring at her, deep sorrow in her eyes.

Standing by her apartment window, Charity pressed her face against the glass. Outside, the evening's dusk had gathered. She should have accepted the Bylers' dinner invitation or gone somewhere else for Thanksgiving.

But where? She had no relatives in the small community, and Holmes County was too far away for a quick visit. Even if she wished to see her old haunts, David would be there. She might run across him with another girl on his arm. What would her reaction be? She might scream and run, or worse, faint. David must have a girlfriend by now. He was too handsome, charming, and kind to remain unattached. When she had been with him, girls had always glanced at her with jealousy.

In her sorrow she had stayed home today. She should at least give thanks that she lived in Nebraska. David's absence would hurt so much worse back in Ohio.

When a buggy appeared in the distance, she stepped back from the glass. Who would be coming at this hour? On Thanksgiving evening, after a hearty dinner, families lingered to enjoy each other's company.

The buggy turned in her driveway, and then she heard the distinct voice of Grandpa Byler call to his horse. "Whoa there."

She forced herself to open the front door.

Grandma Byler was already halfway to the house carrying a food dish. "Goot evening, Charity. How are you? It's a little late. Is it okay if we intrude on your evening for a while?"

"Of course, but I . . . you didn't need to."

"No objections from you," Grandma Byler ordered. "You shouldn't have been alone today, but I understand. Adjusting to a new community takes time. Maybe next year or the Christmas holidays can be spent with our family."

"It's okay," Charity told her.

Grandma Byler paused to wait for her husband, who had finished tying his horse and was hurrying toward them.

They approached together, and Grandpa Byler held out his hand to Charity. "Are you all right? We should have come over earlier and insisted that you join us for dinner today, but we thought you were going to join another family."

"I'm fine," Charity choked out, shaking his hand.

Grandma Byler clucked her tongue. "I know you are suffering, poor girl. We've brought you supper. It's not much, but perhaps a goot meal will help."

"And someone to talk to," Grandpa Byler suggested. "We're just two out-of-touch old people, but we still know how to listen."

Charity ducked her head to compose herself. Their kindness moved her deeply.

Grandma Byler slipped her arm around Charity's shoulder and ushered her inside the house where the food dishes were deposited on the kitchen table. The three seated themselves on the couch in the living room.

"I can't stop crying," Charity said. "I don't mean to burden you with my troubles. You have both been so kind to me and offered me a fresh start, but I can't forget David any more than I can stop painting."

"Perhaps the Lord brought you out here for a reason we don't yet understand," Grandma Byler said. "I know that my heart is not the one which was broken, but sorrows are a part of life. No one is exempt."

"I know. I should be ashamed of myself."

"Tears are the Lord's healing rain," Grandpa Byler told her. "We must never be ashamed of our sorrow. Peace comes after the storm."

"That's just the problem," Charity told him. "At times I think I have found peace, but soon it slips away. Do you really think I can find a fresh start here?"

"You would mean love, no doubt?" Grandma Byler laid her hand on Charity's arm.

Charity stifled a gasp. How had she known?

"Is there a young man looking at you with favor?" Grandma Byler continued.

Charity couldn't answer.

"I am not surprised," Grandpa Byler said. "The Lord does not intend a man or a woman to walk through life alone—except in rare circumstances."

"Even with this pain in their hearts?" Charity asked.

"Time brings healing to the most bruised hearts." Grandma Byler patted Charity's arm.

"You must pray and seek the Lord's will," Grandpa Byler said. "We will do the same, but whatever happens you have our full support. Be assured of that."

Charity leaped to her feet. "I shouldn't be keeping you. Thank you so much for coming."

"We don't have to rush off." Grandma Byler gave her a tender smile.

"Your coming has meant more than you will ever know, but I have taken enough of your time."

"Come, my dear," Grandpa Byler said to his wife. "Charity wishes to be alone. She is a private griever."

"Oh, of course," the older woman answered. She and her husband made their way to the door. "You are always welcome at our house," Grandma Byler said to Charity. "Come anytime you wish to visit. Don't ever forget that."

Charity nodded and waited on the threshold while Grandpa Byler untied his horse and the buggy drove out of the lane. She waved until they disappeared from sight.

Could she open her heart to another man, perhaps a man like James Troyer? A chill crept over her whole body. Charity closed and locked the apartment door. She stood still for a long time, lost in reflection.

10

Wilma fidgeted in her seat on Sunday morning. Grandpa had the main sermon, and he paced slowly in front of the minister's bench.

"There are two ways in this life, and two choices," Grandpa declared, his hands clasped on his chest with the graying beard tucked beneath them. "There is the wrong way and the right way, the broad road and the narrow. The Lord is here to help us make the choice that pleases Him, but we must make the decision."

Wilma moved sideways on the hard, backless bench in search of a more comfortable spot. Twelve o'clock was thirty minutes away. He would preach right up to his allotted time, which meant the service wouldn't wind down until a quarter after twelve. Lunch would be served late again, but spiritual matters came first on Sunday morning. That was how things worked in the community and the way they should work. There were principles that never changed—or did they?

A bitter question swirled in her mind. Why did she not have a date with James tonight when her cinnamon rolls on Thanksgiving Day had been such a success? Even Grandma had found them worthy of comment. "These taste just like my own Mamm's," she had said. "What did you do, Wilma?"

She had smiled and ducked her head. "Nothing much, Grandma. I just took extra care."

Most of the women had chuckled. They approved of her pursuit of James Troyer.

Grandma had given Wilma a hug. "You are talented. There is no question there."

Great joy should have filled her heart after such praise from women who knew the best techniques of baking and cooking. She should have floated across the dining room floor in a daze on Thanksgiving Day. If only James had joined in the congratulations beyond a nonchalant, "They were delicious as usual, Wilma."

To make matters worse, Amos had chatted with Susie throughout the meal while James had avoided her. That night, alone in her room, the tears had burst forth like a summer rain when she had thought about Amos asking Susie for a date. Of course Susie shouldn't have refused Amos's attentions. But why hadn't James sat by Wilma's side and warmed her heart?

There was no sugarcoating it: The day had been a colossal failure.

Grandpa's sermon continued in one ear while Wilma's thoughts swirled. There could be only one reason why James had ignored her. She had been trying not to glance in Charity's direction, but she could resist no longer. Wilma allowed herself to peer at the other woman from the corner of her eye.

Charity was focused on Grandpa, but Wilma knew that the teacher would not stare at a man during a sermon. James, on the other hand, seemed to have no such compunctions. James had a clear line of sight from across the room, where he was seated in the unmarried men's section. His gaze was fixed on Charity, a dreamy expression on his face. Charity and her paintings were to blame for Wilma's failure, for her humiliation, and for the wreckage of her plans.

Wilma forced herself to look away, her eyes burning. How could she have been so wrong? How could the ways of the community have led her so far astray? James was in love—madly from the look of things—and Charity couldn't bake cinnamon rolls for any man, let alone her husband. James had to know this. Or was love really so blind? James should know better than to fall in love with illusions, with paintings, with things that would not provide for his needs.

Grandpa's voice cut into Wilma's thoughts. "The Lord will help us each and every day," he proclaimed.

How will He? she almost shouted to Grandpa, but this was a church service. No one spoke during the sermon. Couldn't Grandpa see that his preaching was not helping her? Didn't he understand that the ground under her feet was giving way? Why did the Lord not come to her aid? She had been faithful and done her duty.

Could it be that complete success wasn't possible? Had Wilma set her sights too high? Amos was properly impressed with Susie, and that was half the battle. She would rather suffer than her cousin. Susie had avoided her after Thanksgiving dinner, and the bakery had been closed on Friday. There had been no chance to tell Susie that she held nothing against her. Amos would take Susie home for a Sunday evening date, and she was glad. Susie belonged with Amos, as she knew she belonged with James.

Wilma glanced in James's direction again. He was still watching Charity, who had to notice the attention. Any girl would feel that handsome gaze on her face and know that a great love was within her grasp. Charity would not pass on the opportunity to snag a husband like James. No girl would!

"Now let us come to prayer," Grandpa Byler announced, concluding his sermon.

The congregation kneeled at their benches.

Help James see his mistake before he takes Charity home on a date, Wilma prayed fervently.

If that prayer wasn't answered, her humiliation would be complete. She should have been more discreet in her pursuit of the man. But who would have guessed her failure? Hadn't the community rejected Charity's painting at the auction? That day seemed so distant. Charity had climbed a long hill to catch the most eligible bachelor in the community.

With a rustling of feet the congregation took their seats, and after the testimonies, the last song began. Wilma kept her gaze on the page. Charity would be smiling at James since Grandpa's sermon was finished. Her heart must be pounding with joy. Wilma swallowed hard. She had tried her best and failed. She would have to settle for someone else after all.

The song ended and Wilma rose. She followed the other girls into the kitchen while the men assembled the tables in the living room for lunch.

Susie bumped into her shoulder in the tight quarters and leaned over to whisper, "I have to confess something. I feel so guilty that I didn't tell you on Thursday after dinner, but I just couldn't bring myself to say the words."

Wilma nodded. "It's okay. I overheard the conversation."

"What are we to do?" Susie clutched her elbow.

"You will go home with him, as you have agreed to do. I don't begrudge you," Wilma said.

Susie appeared grateful for her understanding, and there was something else in her cousin's eyes—sorrow for her misfortune.

Nothing made sense! Nothing!

That Sunday evening at the hymn singing, the grandfather clock in the hallway struck nine. The last strains of the parting hymn, "Blest Be the Tie That Binds," still hung in the air.

Susie closed the hymnal and snuck another glance across the room.

Amos gave her a warm smile, and dizzy circles raced around her heart. In a few moments she would be seated beside him on his buggy seat. They would race into the darkness with the drum of horse's hooves ahead of them. Amos would have a fast horse. She knew he would. Amos wasn't capable of driving a plodding horse like Mamm's and Daett's. The evening was warm for a late November night. She would leave the buggy door open and allow the air to blow over their faces. Hers would be flushed. Happiness would fill her heart to overflowing. This was her first date, and with a wunderbah man like Amos.

Susie's glance shifted to the other side of the room. Clyde was staring at her. She had almost forgotten about him. Certainly he didn't know about her date with Amos. But he would soon. The whole community would know when she climbed into Amos's buggy.

Would Clyde be angry? Would he think she had led him down the fairy path when he paid that horrendous price for her sticky buns at the school auction? Surely not. She hadn't made any promises. He had to know there was competition, especially since the Troyer brothers had moved into the community. There was no shame in accepting a date with Amos. Clyde would have made an excellent husband, but she couldn't marry out of pity. She had to take the best choice available to her.

Out of the corner of her eye, Susie saw Amos stand and leave the room. She didn't dare look at him directly. Not with Clyde's gaze fixed on her.

Wilma was the one who truly suffered. Wilma deserved her full sympathy and more. Wilma was a jewel. Why couldn't James see that? Wilma was smiling bravely, seated on the front bench, even as he stood to follow his brother out the door. Wilma should have been the one on a date tonight.

Susie froze. Did Charity have a date with James tonight? The brothers often did things together. She could never enjoy her evening with Amos if she knew that at the same time James sat on Charity's living room couch instead of Wilma's.

Susie lunged to her feet and hurried out of the room. She grabbed her shawl in the washroom to arrive breathless at Amos's buggy.

"Goot evening," he greeted her with a bright smile. "What an honor to take home the best cook in the community."

"Amos," she scolded. "Wilma is the best cook. You know that."

He chuckled and hopped into the buggy with her. "You know I have reasons for taking you home other than your goot cooking."

"I had hoped so." Susie gathered the nerve for a quick sideways glance. His handsome face, so near, made her heart pound.

They whirled out of the driveway in the darkness. He did have a fast horse. She had never ridden at this speed. The passing trees were a blur.

"Forgive the dashing horse," he said. "I haven't had time to train West Wind properly. I left my goot horse back in Wisconsin. He was fast and safe, which was why my cousin offered such a tidy sum. I couldn't afford the cost of transporting the horse to Nebraska. Not at that price."

She clung to the side of the buggy with one hand. "Your horse in Wisconsin was fast?"

She could hear the grin in his voice. "You could actually enjoy his speed, knowing he wouldn't shy or veer off suddenly, but yah, he was faster than this. Why?"

"I suppose I'm used to Daett's old plodder."

His laughter filled the night. "My guess is your Daett had his fast horses in his day. Every Amish boy dreams of the time when he finds a goot horse at a price he can afford."

Susie remembered how Clyde had spent $600 to eat sticky

buns with her. She suppressed the awful thought, reminding herself what a great honor it was to ride with Amos's fast horse in the buggy traces.

"Didn't he?" Amos glanced at her.

"I-I have never heard Daett mention a fast horse," Susie stammered.

"Well, he probably wouldn't. Men get that way when they are older. Ashamed of their wild ways."

"Have you had wild times?"

He snorted. "Not really. Just fast horses. Wisconsin's *Rumspringa* was pretty tame. How about you?"

"I live in Nebraska. How wild can that be?"

"Things weren't that different for us. Do you live at the second house down?"

"Yah."

"Sorry, I should know even in the darkness." He steered the horse into the driveway at a sharp angle.

She gripped the side of the buggy tighter. "I understand. You're new to the community."

"Whoa there." He tugged back on the reins. They ended up at the hitching rack in a flourish of leather and sliding hooves. He jumped out immediately to tie his horse.

She waited a moment to catch her breath and slow the beat of her heart. She could get used to this. But she still wondered if James had taken Charity home from the hymn singing. She had to find out.

"Are you coming?" Amos offered his hand. "It's safe to get down."

Susie took his hand, found the step with one foot, and leaped to the ground.

His hand stayed in hers as they headed up the sidewalk to the house, where a kerosene lamp glowed warmly in the living room window.

Charity released her horse into the pasture through the fence gate. She had driven aimlessly around the community back roads since the close of the hymn singing, knowing what awaited her inside the small apartment—loneliness, questions, regrets, and agonies from the past.

She steadied herself against the fence post, then walked up to the front door and opened it. She found a match in the desk drawer and lit the lamp. She had wanted David by her side tonight at the hymn singing. Instead, James had watched her the whole evening. He had done the same at the Sunday morning service. Was James enamored with her, perhaps falling in love?

She settled into her couch with a groan and stared at the flickering shadows on the living room ceiling. There would never be another man like David. But should she cling to his memory? She could not change what had happened to their engagement. The tattered edges lay at her feet along with her broken heart. Did James offer her an opportunity for a fresh start, the one Grandpa Byler had alluded to on Thanksgiving? She wished he had been more specific, but her reaction had been to hustle him and his Frau out of her living room.

Perhaps Grandpa Byler didn't know, or wouldn't have told her even if she had asked. Such things were matters of the heart, which even church leaders were hesitant to touch. Maybe nobody knew the answer, but if James was interested in her—and he obviously was—she must at least prepare an answer for him. The memory of David's love might always linger in her life, like a delicate perfume, too expensive to find again and too precious to forget. Could James live with that? Could she?

If James asked to drive them home for a date, most girls would settle without question. That she even considered turning him down would be a scandal in itself. What little reputation she had here would be gone forever. Painting would no longer seem like a curious hobby but the road to insanity.

Why was it that she seemed doomed in love? Charity would give her ability to paint any day for David's affections, but that hadn't been enough for David's Daett. "Once a painter, always a painter," the bishop had roared on the front porch that day. "The heart cannot be changed."

So how did David's Daett expect her heart to change when it came to loving his son? The contradiction had never been addressed by the bishop—if he even cared. Reputation was Bishop Zook's first concern. She had soiled the community's precious *Ordnung* by her actions.

Charity stood and paced the floor. Could she open her heart again, perhaps just a sliver? James didn't know her past, but he knew about her paintings and still seemed interested. Wasn't that worth a try? He might not be David, but he would be a goot husband. He would love her, and the Lord knew she needed love. Just a man's warm hand wrapped around hers, with his comforting presence seated beside her on the couch, would be a balm to her stricken soul.

She lifted the kerosene lamp from the desk. The time was late, and she couldn't think anymore.

"Good night, David," she whispered, "my forever and ever, true sweetheart."

And then she slipped through her bedroom door.

11

In the predawn darkness of the following Monday morning, Wilma entered the bakery and lit the gas lantern.

She hung the lantern on its ceiling hook, then stepped back to survey the empty bakery. Everything was spotless, exactly as they had left things Wednesday evening, but so much had changed since then. The whole community would awaken to the news that Amos Troyer had taken Susie Mast home on a Sunday evening date.

Wilma had left the hymn singing right after Susie. The effort to keep smiling was too much. Once she was safely inside her bedroom, the tears had come in a flood. Not only had she been rejected, but James might have driven Charity home for their first date. That was the real reason she had rushed away. Seeing Charity climb into James's buggy would have been too much. In retrospect, however, she should have faced it. The verification of her suspicions this morning would twist her heart even worse.

She had tossed and turned in bed last night, dreading the moment, seeing clearly what might have happened. James, sitting on Charity's living room couch, would have cast the same cow eyes at her as he had at the singing, while a painting sat in the corner instead of delicious baked goodies on the dining room table. Charity would have sat happily smiling beside him, reveling in her conquest. James had completely lost his goot sense, and Wilma could do nothing about it.

Surely Susie would know whether James had driven Charity home from the hymn singing. Amos would have shared the news of his brother's date, even if she hadn't dared ask point-blank. At least Susie was still on her side, and Susie would always be there for her. This was a time of darkness, of trouble and shame. She must be strong and triumphant.

The door creaked open, and Wilma whirled about. "Susie!" She rushed over to her.

"Oh, Wilma! I'm so sorry."

The two clung to each other.

"Did James take that awful woman home?" Wilma held her cousin at arm's length.

Susie shook her head. "James came home soon after we did and slipped upstairs after a quick greeting for us."

"Then there is hope. I must tell myself this and not despair. If James hasn't jumped over the cliff, he must be having second thoughts. So tell me, how was your time with Amos? Great, I assume."

Susie's face flushed. "It was. We had a goot time."

"Don't downplay your victory," Wilma scolded. "I know it was wunderbah—marvelous in fact. The Troyer brothers are the cream of the crop. Did Amos ask for another date?"

Susie nodded, her face still flaming. "I'm so sorry that you are out of this."

"Nonsense. I have no one to blame but myself. Now I have a little breathing room, perhaps a small window of hope. I must plan how to get James's attention. I must show him what a mistake Charity is. Paintings!" Wilma threw her hands skyward. "What comfort are paintings in a man's life?"

"Amos said the Troyer family so enjoyed Thanksgiving at your place that they are returning the favor. We are all invited to breakfast on Christmas morning when several of their relatives visit from Wisconsin."

Wilma clapped her hands. "Thank the Lord for His mercy. This is my answer, my chance, if I can impress the relatives from Wisconsin. With your foot already in the Troyers' door, James can't help but see me in the best light."

"You know I will help, but I am still troubled about this."

"No time for doubt," Wilma said. "I know what you are thinking. James is enamored with Charity. What hope do I have? James was gazing at her on Sunday the same way he gazes at this painting. But a painting is fantasy, and James is seeing a fantasy when he looks at Charity. I must break through the fog with the practical things in life that every man needs."

"I will do what I can, but once a man becomes fascinated with a woman, it's hard to change his mind."

"We've already been over that," Wilma said with a dismissive wave. "Let's get busy. An idea will come to me. I must bake something big. On second thought, maybe not so big. I need the ordinary done in an extraordinary way. That's how I succeeded on Thanksgiving."

"I hope it works," Susie mumbled. "Amos said they won't be stopping by anymore. With winter coming on fast, their carpentry work leaves no extra time."

Wilma took a deep breath. "Okay. We both know there's more to it than that, but this might be for the best. So we have until Christmas to produce the maximum impact. We will take our usual baked goods. Should we add a cake perhaps? Something simple but eye-catching."

"You'll think of something. Christmas is still a few weeks away."

"Keep your ears open. Amos might drop some hint, some family favorite that James loves."

Susie nodded. "I will, but I am still sorry that Amos asked me for a date first."

"It's not your fault." Wilma gave Susie a quick hug. "But I can imagine how awful I'd feel if the roles were reversed. In the meantime, we are going to win this battle. There is no way a painting is going to steal a man from Wilma Wengerd. So tell me about your evening with Amos. We will comfort ourselves with hope and goot news."

Susie smiled. She had greatly enjoyed her time with Amos, and Wilma was right that being positive about the situation was better than mulling in despair.

Grandpa burst through the bakery door. "Goot morning. I heard the goot news, Susie. Congratulations!" He grinned and swept her into a bear hug.

Susie blushed deeply. "Thank you, Grandpa."

Grandpa chuckled. "I just had to check if a celebration was going on this morning. Perhaps coffee and doughnuts with the Troyer brothers?"

"It's a little early for that," Wilma told him. "We haven't started our baking."

"I guess so," Grandpa said. "May I sit down?"

Susie hurried to bring him a chair.

He settled in with a sigh. "Sorry. Weary bones in the morning. So how was your evening with Amos? Your very first date, yah?"

Susie felt her face warm and dropped her gaze. There was no way she was going to tell Grandpa how she felt gazing into Amos's handsome face, having him so close to her on the buggy seat and later on the living room couch.

Grandpa smiled. "It was goot, I see. You can't go wrong with Amos. Will you be seeing him again?"

"Yah," Susie whispered.

Grandpa sobered as he faced Wilma. "I haven't forgotten you

or the sorrow that must be on your heart. How are you taking this? I know you had your hopes set on James."

"I still do," Wilma replied firmly. "Hope is not dead."

"I don't know about that," Grandpa said. "James should have taken you home on a date before his brother did—if he planned to."

Wilma raised her chin but didn't answer.

"Will this cause a rift between the two of you?" Grandpa asked.

Wilma waved dismissively. "You don't have to worry about me getting jealous of Susie. Not for one minute."

"I didn't quite mean it in that way." He frowned. "I hope there is no bitterness in your heart toward Charity."

Susie realized that this was the reason for Grandpa's early visit. "Can I get you some coffee?"

He focused on Susie for a second. "Coffee would be great. Thank you."

She hurried to the back room. She filled the kettle with water and lit the burner, trying to give Wilma and Grandpa some privacy, but she could still hear them in the early morning quiet.

"Charity is not winning this battle," Wilma said.

"You must prepare yourself for whomever James might choose, Wilma dear," Grandpa said. "Everyone must submit to the Lord's will. Perhaps this is Charity's chance at a new beginning after her past troubles."

"I don't care what troubles she's had," Wilma snapped. "Charity has no right to upset the old ways with her paintings."

He sighed. "This is becoming more complicated than I had imagined, and I'm sorry that you are caught in the middle of it. Perhaps the Lord wishes to teach us that things are not always how they appear. One thing I do know is that there should not be a battle between the two of you over a man."

Wilma huffed almost defiantly. "You don't expect me to sit by while Charity waltzes in here and steals the man I want. The girl can't cook. All she can do is paint."

"And teach school."

"Anyone can do that. James will come to his senses, hopefully before it's too late."

"Wilma," he chided. "Charity is not what you think she is, and if James decides that Charity is the best Frau for him, you must accept his choice. Don't become bitter. You can have any man you want in the community."

"Except James Troyer."

The whistle of the teakettle drowned out Grandpa's reply, but from the look on Wilma's face when Susie carried in Grandpa's coffee, the conversation hadn't proceeded to any satisfactory conclusion.

He drew a long breath over his coffee. "This is perfect. You know how to make goot coffee."

"That's because she doesn't waste her time with silly things like painting." Wilma's remark cut the air.

He ignored it and turned to Susie. "What do you think about Charity's painting?"

"Charity can paint," Susie allowed. "But then I don't know much about painting."

"What do you think of Charity?"

"She shouldn't take James away from Wilma."

"What if Charity isn't taking James away from Wilma?"

Wilma snorted. "Then what are we talking about?"

"What if Charity isn't sure she wants James's attentions?"

Wilma's laugh was harsh. "What dream world are you in, Grandpa?"

Susie cleared her throat. "From what I can see, Charity isn't rejecting the man. In fact, Charity is much like her paintings—distant, demure, and alluring."

"I thought you didn't know anything about paintings?"

"I don't."

"Thank the Lord someone sees the truth," Wilma declared. "You should join us in helping James see the danger he is in."

Grandpa grimaced. "There is more going on than you girls realize. Charity has had her heartaches. You should take that into consideration."

"Maybe," Susie said.

"The woman is a man stealer, straight up and down, without question," Wilma snapped. "She is using her beauty and her painting ability to snare a goot man into a life of hunger and emptiness. Charity barely knows what an oven is, let alone how to bake for a man or her family or her Kinner. You should be on our side, Grandpa. I'll say it again."

"I am, but that doesn't leave Charity outside of our care and concern."

Wilma got up and stalked into the kitchen. "After I am safely married to James, I will feel plenty of care and concern for Charity. Now, we are way behind schedule, Grandpa, if you don't mind."

"I'm sorry," he said and gulped down his coffee.

"You shouldn't have been so short with him," Susie told Wilma after Grandpa left. "He was trying to help, and you were disrespectful."

Wilma's eyes blazed. "Grandpa, of all people, should see how serious this is! He's a preacher and a bishop. He's allowing Charity's charm to blind his eyes just like James. But I don't want to talk about this anymore. I have a headache. Tell me about your evening with Amos. We never got to that subject."

Susie didn't answer, and Wilma didn't insist. The joy from her evening with Amos had vanished.

"I'm taking Grandpa and Grandma doughnuts when they are done," Susie finally said.

Wilma nodded, her anger calmed. "I was a little short with him. You can tell him I'm sorry."

"It's understandable," Susie told her.

The dawn grew in the sky outside as they worked silently, and the heat of the ovens crept through the bakery.

Late that evening, Charity was busy at the counter, slicing vegetables for soup. She jumped when a soft knock sounded on her front door. No buggy had driven in, but she had been occupied. Cooking took her full focus.

She wiped her hands on her apron and walked over to open the door a crack. "Goot evening."

"Charity," James answered.

She gasped.

"Sorry if I startled you," he said. "May I come in?"

"You shouldn't be here."

"Why not?"

For a thousand reasons, she wanted to say. But she nonetheless remained silent.

"Am I being rejected at the doorstep?"

She opened the door and tried to smile. "I'm making vegetable soup. If you care to wait, I can serve you supper."

"We were working late, and I've already eaten. I won't keep you long." He took off his hat and ran his hand through his hair.

"Are you here to see the painting again?"

James grinned. "I would love that, but no. I came to ask if you would consider letting me drive you home on Sunday evening for a date."

"James!" she exclaimed. "You don't know what you are asking."

"I think I know my own mind," he said. "And Amos took Susie

home on Sunday evening. We can't have the younger brother running rings around the older."

"Is that why you are asking me?"

Alarm filled his face. "Absolutely not! I was teasing. I ask because I care about you. I think I have from the first time I laid eyes on you. What man wouldn't be impressed with you? In fact, I can't believe you aren't seeing someone."

"There is a reason." She avoided his gaze.

"You are available?" He sounded worried. "You're not writing to someone back in Holmes County?"

She looked away. Her eyes filled, and soon he would notice. "I'm available. That's not the problem."

"You would not consider me then?"

"James, please," she begged. "Any girl would consider you."

His relief showed. "Is that a yah, then?"

"I have to think about this. Can you give me some time?"

"But you had to know that I care for you. Are you having doubts about me?"

"It's not you. It's me. But I can't explain right now."

He appeared confused. "I can wait. Not that I want to, but I would wait a long time for you, Charity Lynn Martin."

He had to see the tears this time.

"That's very kind of you."

He reached for her hand. "Have I offended you? Have I done something I shouldn't have?"

Charity shook her head. "Do you want to see the painting?"

He smiled and followed her. She drew back the sheet, and he stood transfixed for a long time.

"It is still amazing. I should be going," he finally said. "So you will let me know when you decide?"

She nodded.

He slipped out of the house as quietly as he had come.

Charity peeked out from behind the drapes by the front window to watch him drive his buggy down the lane. She had opened her heart a sliver—otherwise she would have given him a firm no. But what had she done? Waves of fear raced through her. She had betrayed David, even if they could never be.

12

Wilma awakened at her usual time on Christmas morning and tiptoed downstairs. Mamm and Daett were still sleeping, but she needed to bake the angel food cake for the Troyers' Christmas Day breakfast celebration. There had been time yesterday after they had closed the bakery, but she wanted every advantage. A day-old cake was not a risk worth taking.

"The Troyers said we don't need to take anything," Mamm had reminded her last night. "You can sleep in tomorrow morning."

Which meant that the last thing she would do was create a disturbance in the kitchen. The Wengerd family members were light sleepers. Beating an angel food cake into the heavenly excellence she needed would create plenty of noise. The bakery was the only place to work at four thirty in the morning, so Wilma pulled on her coat and stepped outside.

The air was brisk, with the distant horizon still dark, the stars bright across the whole stretch of visible sky. Multicolored lights twinkled in the living room windows of the English homes. A snow squall had rolled through the community in the early morning hours, and the ground was covered with a fluffy whiteness. Christmas Day would dawn with a glorious brightness. Everything was perfect for the moment when she would once more impress upon James the importance of home, family, goot cooking, and a Frau who could supply those things.

James must have his doubts about Charity's fitness. Otherwise he would have taken her home on a Sunday evening date by this time.

Wilma had waited with bated breath at each Sunday evening hymn singing. What if this was the night Charity followed James out to his buggy? Her humiliation was already great. There were whispers at the youth gatherings ever since Susie had started dating Amos, and Wilma was still unattached. Everyone had figured out the extent of her failure, and the general consensus was that James had changed his mind about Wilma.

James's adoring gaze was fixed on Charity during most of the services, so the connection was natural. But Wilma refused to leave the hymn singings early again. The truth must be faced when it happened. One night of sleepless torment, not knowing what news the morning would bring, had been enough. She should be in the depths of despair, yet hope hung by a thin thread that refused to break.

"Angel food cake," Susie had reported last week. "James loves angel food cake."

So angel food cake it would be. The egg whites must be beaten to perfection, until the arms ached from exhaustion, but that was okay. James would know how much effort she had expended and get the message. Charity was not the Frau for him. Surely a man would not deprive himself of his favorite cake over his fascination with a painting.

Wilma approached the bakery and stopped her fast pace. Why was there a light in the window? Was Susie inside? This was not a workday. Had she carelessly left a light on the evening before?

She ran the last hundred yards to the bakery door and burst inside.

Susie greeted her with a smile. "Goot morning."

"Why are you here?"

"To help with the angel food cake. I know you didn't bake it last night."

Wilma gave her cousin a long hug. "You are such a dear to think of me. How sweet of you."

"You would do the same for me. We'll trade off beating the egg whites. That way we'll be done in no time."

Wilma wiped away a tear. "I don't deserve this kindness."

"I am the one who doesn't deserve what is happening to me," Susie protested. "Here I'm dating Amos while you are ignored. How could I sleep in this morning while you labored away, trying to open James's eyes?"

She pulled herself together. "Has Amos said anything more? Something you haven't told me?"

Susie shook her head. "We don't talk about Charity or her paintings."

"Then James is having doubts?"

"We're only guessing. We don't know."

"But we do know how to make angel food cake, and we know that James loves it."

"I'll do the first round," Susie offered. "We should keep up the pace back to back, so there isn't a pause."

Wilma began to separate eggs into a bowl. She couldn't hold back the questions. "Dating Amos must be a wunderbah experience, having him sit beside you on the couch each Sunday evening. Does he hold your hand?"

Susie winced. "If the angel food cake doesn't work, I can tell Amos we must stop seeing each other."

"You will do no such thing!" Wilma shot back. "You should not spoil your joy because of my sorrow."

"But when you are scorned by his brother . . . how could I wed the man knowing how miserable you are?"

Wilma shook her head. "I will not have it, and I am not defeated yet. James hasn't taken Charity home from the hymn singing. That's a great victory in itself. Besides, Amos is not to blame for his brother's choices, and he should not be punished for them."

Susie reached for the bowl of egg whites. "Let me."

Wilma gave in with a sigh and walked over to the window. She was already weary.

Susie whipped the egg whites behind her. "It's going to be a beautiful day, I think."

Wilma returned to the counter. "I know, but I'm not too cheerful. My turn."

They kept at it until stiff peaks finally formed.

"Let it never be said that we didn't try," Susie muttered as she gathered the other ingredients they would need.

"To the two cousins and to victory." Wilma waved their whisk in the air, but the heaviness on her heart wouldn't lift.

At nine thirty Susie sat in the back of Mamm and Daett's buggy on their way to the Troyers' for Christmas Day breakfast. Daett's horse, Midnight, plodded along as if they had the whole day to arrive.

"There's no hurry." Daett glanced over the backseat to tease, as if he had read Susie's thoughts. "You already have the man snagged."

"Don't torment her," Mamm scolded. "This is a sensitive time in a girl's life."

"Seems like Susie has done quite well for herself." He sounded pleased. "She's dating one of the Troyer brothers."

"Did you ever have a fast horse in your younger days?" Susie asked, suddenly remembering Amos's claim.

Daett laughed. "Whoa there. Where did that come from?"

"Amos says you probably did."

"Is this the kind of thing you talk about on your dates?"

"You haven't answered my question."

Daett chuckled. "Maybe you had better ask your Mamm. My opinion might be biased."

"Did he?" Susie asked obediently.

Mamm's face was grim. "The man scared me so badly that I almost didn't ride with him again."

Daett grinned from ear to ear as they turned slowly into the Troyers' driveway.

Mamm twisted around in her seat. "If you are worried about fast horses, I'm sure Amos will settle down into a stable and steady husband just like your Daett did."

Susie forced a smile. That was not her worry in the least.

"Why were you down at the bakery this morning?" Mamm asked, still leaning over the backseat.

Daett lurched to a stop, and they hopped out of the buggy.

"I helped Wilma bake an angel food cake," Susie told Mamm on their way up the walk.

Mamm gave her a puzzled frown.

Amos met them at the front door with a twinkle in his eye. "Goot morning. What lovely ladies have arrived on our porch?"

"Goot morning, Amos." Mamm smiled. "No wonder you have my daughter charmed."

"Susie is the one who has won my heart," he assured her.

Mamm shook his hand. "Thanks so much for the invitation this morning."

"You are welcome." Amos motioned her through the front door. "Mamm is inside with Wilma's family. I'd like a moment with Susie, if that's okay."

"Of course." Mamm didn't hesitate.

Amos winked when the door closed behind Mamm.

"You have me blushing all sorts of colors," Susie admonished.

"That is when you are at your best," Amos retorted. "Those colors are lovely on you. Thanks for helping with the angel food cake this morning. Wilma told us the tale of your labors at the bakery. That was a nice gesture."

"You know that is for your brother's benefit." Susie hadn't dared to bring up the subject before.

"I thought it was for me," he teased.

Susie laughed along with him.

"All the same, thanks. James is a little taken with Charity at the moment, but I assume you know that."

"Is James in the house with Wilma?"

Amos shook his head. "He's upstairs changing, but he was impressed with the cake. I hope it tastes as goot as it looks."

"Do you still doubt my baking skills?"

He chuckled. "I never have."

"Oh, Amos." She wanted to melt into his arms, but this was the Troyers' front porch, not the couch in her family's living room on a Sunday evening.

"I have to tend to the horses." He motioned to the barn. "You want to come along?"

"I-I should see if the women need help in the kitchen."

He nodded and headed down the porch steps.

Susie watched Amos go, wishing she had gone with him. She wouldn't really be needed in the kitchen with all the women who were already there, but she couldn't display affection toward Amos at the Troyers' house before James came to his senses. Wilma was hurt enough.

Susie opened the front door, and the display of fried eggs, bacon, pancakes, fresh bread, butter, jams, and a large plate of ham on the dining room table greeted her. The Troyer family had spared no effort to welcome their guests and relatives.

Susie entered the crowded kitchen, and several women greeted her.

"Can I help?" Susie offered.

Amos's Mamm, Lydia, gave her a kind smile. "We are almost done, but thank you for offering. The men will be in any minute, and the last pan of pancakes are almost made. We have to eat before things get cold."

Susie caught sight of Wilma and drifted over to her. "How did things go this morning with the cake? Amos seemed impressed."

Wilma gave her a grim expression. "James was quite pleased, but he didn't stay around. Pulling him back from the abyss will be difficult, but I guess I knew that."

"We tried our best," Susie whispered.

"The men are here," Lydia announced. "Let's move out to the dining room."

Susie stayed close to Wilma's side until they were seated at the table. Amos sent her a wink and James gave Wilma a quick smile. Perhaps their plan would work in spite of Wilma's doubts.

The sun was still in the sky that evening when James's buggy pulled into Charity's driveway. She left her pot of lentil soup on the stove and met him at the door with her hands fluttering. "You are early. We said six or seven."

He grinned. "That's a broad range of time. But thanks for passing me the note last Sunday evening. That was a sweet way of letting me know I could come over."

"This is not a date," Charity told him firmly, "and it's not even five o'clock. I don't have supper ready."

"Then I will help you cook. Or I'll sit and watch you work. Believe me, this is a great privilege, you allowing me to visit you."

"You don't know what you are getting into."

James laughed. "Are you wanted for murder?"

She managed to laugh along with him, but he was right in a way. She had killed David's heart with her paintings. Was that not the root of this whole problem? "I can't cook. Surely you know that by now."

"Why does that matter?" he asked. "And the community gossip sometimes exaggerates things."

"They don't exaggerate. I am a disaster when it comes to cooking and baking."

"I don't see smoke pouring from the kitchen stove."

"Don't say that, please. I have soup on the stove. That's about the extent of my ability. I can only imagine the breakfast your Mamm served this morning."

"You are worried about Wilma and her baking skills. That's the real problem, right?"

She wrung her hands. "Wilma and Susie are among the best cooks in the community. So why are you here?"

"Because you said I could come."

"We are going around in circles, and I haven't made my soup yet." She raced back to the kitchen stove.

He followed and took the spoon from her hand. "Let me help."

"You know how to cook?"

"Enough not to starve."

"That's more than me," Charity moaned under her breath.

He glanced at her sideways. "Did your Mamm never teach you?"

"She let me paint."

"Well, you could still learn."

"I don't know. I'm old."

He laughed. "Not that old."

"Why do you insist on this?"

"Maybe there are things in life more important than food."

She turned her face away. "You can't be real."

"Does your boyfriend back in Holmes County know you can't cook?"

"I told you, I don't have a boyfriend."

"You had a boyfriend."

"How do you know?"

"I guessed. What happened?"

"Do we have to discuss this?"

"We should. You seem haunted by it."

Charity reached for the spoon. "I should be doing the cooking. That's the woman's place in the home."

"The soup is done," he said.

"Then we should eat since you are here."

"Where are the bowls and utensils?"

"In the cupboard."

James laid his hand on her arm. "It's okay. Whatever happened wasn't your fault."

A lump formed in her throat. "You don't know what you are talking about."

"Are we going to argue all night?"

"You are the one who insisted on coming."

"You could have told me not to."

"Maybe I'm lonesome on Christmas." The tears ran freely, and she couldn't hide them.

His voice was tender. "You are a wunderbah woman, one I long to know better. Shall we eat?"

She nodded and he carried the pot of soup to the table. He bowed his head and gave thanks. She reached for his hand and wrapped her fingers around his until he finished the prayer and said, "Amen."

13

The blasts from the late January wind blew across the prairie, pushing against Wilma's coat. In the predawn darkness, clouds scurried across the skies. Wilma ran the last few yards to the bakery door and paused to catch her breath on the stoop. She struggled with the doorknob and saw there was a thin layer of ice around the door. Her mittens slipped twice before she broke the seal of ice with a final push of her shoulder. The door slammed shut behind her.

The cold darkness of the interior greeted her. She fumbled with a match and lit the lantern. The light did little to drive away the gloom or the cold. Not that long ago the bakery had been a cheerful place, a refuge, a comfort that spoke of the future, of family and Kinner, and a husband to walk by her side. Now hope had been cruelly wrenched from her heart. The community buzzed with the news that James's buggy had been spotted at Charity's place on Christmas Day, the very evening of the day when James had eaten her angel food cake and had proclaimed it delicious, worthy of the highest praise.

How long had the man been sneaking over to Charity's place? This explained why James wasn't taking Charity home on Sunday evenings. They were already seeing each other in secret. James must be ashamed of himself. There could be no other explanation, yet he couldn't stay away from Charity's charms. Wilma's best efforts had failed to persuade James of his folly.

She paced the cold bakery floor as she waited for Susie. Her cousin's presence would comfort, but the distance between them continued to grow, even as they tried their best to prevent the fissure. They were bound by family and friendship. Nothing could change that, yet they were changing. Amos drove Susie home for their regular date on Sunday evenings while Wilma rode home with her younger brothers. Susie's sympathy could not ease the hurt of James's rejection.

Everyone now knew that Charity had James's attention securely in her apron pocket. How had she managed to capture his heart? The man couldn't take his eyes off her at the Sunday services. James always made sure he sat on the front bench at the hymn singings for a better view. At least Charity had the decency to stay a row back. So why didn't he make their relationship official and drive her home on Sunday evenings like normal couples? The community's teacher was expected to set an example. Was she exempt from the norms? With her paintings, she had already succeeded in shattering long-held customs. The woman was about to destroy the community, and everyone, including Grandpa, was too blind to notice.

Wilma wanted to crawl in some deep, dark hole like a groundhog and not come out until spring. Maybe things would make sense by then. They could shut down the bakery for the winter, but Grandpa had always kept the place open for two days a week while the snow flew. She was not like Charity. Wilma maintained traditions, even when her heart was ripped to shreds. They would not let Grandpa down.

She approached the bakery window and glanced down the lane toward the main road. Where was Susie? It was unlike her to be late. Had she forgotten this was Thursday morning? Maybe the whole world was in turmoil, and it would never settle down again.

Sighing, Wilma returned to the counter. She might as well get busy. Susie would come when she could, with a perfectly goot explanation for her tardiness. She couldn't doubt her cousin. If Charity succeeded in sowing discord between Wilma and Susie on top of stealing James's heart, Wilma might never recover.

After slipping on a white apron, she wiped her eyes with the edge of the cloth. What had gone so wrong? How could this have happened? Somehow Charity, the painter, had become the respected schoolteacher who dated James Troyer.

Wilma gave into her hurt and wept. Why had Grandpa brought Charity into the community and approved of her? His purchase of her painting at the school auction must have established in everyone's mind that her talents had value. What else explained the lack of outcry at Charity's conquest of the community's most eligible bachelor? Surely others had to connect the dots. Were the parents of her students not worried about the subliminal message being taught to their daughters? Charity's life screamed, "Don't worry about keeping house and caring for your family. Go to the English for painting lessons, and your husband will be the most handsome man in the community."

Wilma looked toward the heavens. Did the Lord even care? Wasn't He interested in these things? Didn't God reward hard work and faithfulness? James was fully aware of it all—her baking skills, her housekeeping abilities, her faithfulness to the community's traditions—but nothing had made an impression.

Charity had a prettier face. Maybe that was what had captured his attention. Men were like that, but she had always believed they came to their senses before they took the sacred wedding vows. It seemed real life would contradict that prediction. Her faith was shaken.

Where was Susie? Wilma was not about to stir up the first batch of sticky buns until Susie arrived. If she began, she couldn't stop until the dough was laid out to rise.

She would go to Susie's house and find her. The first customers didn't arrive early in the wintertime anyway. Wilma wrapped her coat tight around her shoulders and rushed out again into the blast of the wind.

Susie hurried up the lane from the Masts' home. She was late, but the storm was no excuse. Wilma would be disturbed and for a goot reason. Grandpa's house had a light on, and so did the bakery. She hastened her steps down the road.

Grandpa called from his front door, "Susie, is that you?"

"Yah." She stopped, and the wind blasted into her face.

"Can you come in?" He sounded worried.

She ran into the lane and up the front porch steps. "What is wrong?"

"Praise be the Lord!" he proclaimed. "Finally someone has come."

"What is it?" She reached for his cold hand. "You are outside without a coat."

"Can you stay with Grandma? It's bad. I have to call for the ambulance."

"What happened?" Susie's blood pounded in her ears.

"She fell going down the front steps. I think her leg is broken." His voice failed him for a moment. "Can you stay with her until I place the call?"

"In this weather? The phone shack is a quarter mile down the road."

"I have to go," Grandpa said.

"I'm going," she said firmly. "I am dressed for the weather."

Relief filled his face. "Thank you."

"Yah, now go back to Grandma." She laid her hand on his arm. "I'll hurry."

Grandpa retreated inside, and the door closed.

Susie ran into the wind, ignoring its harsh lashes against her face. She stumbled but righted herself to arrive breathless at the phone shack. She opened the creaking door and yanked the receiver off the hook. How was she to dial in the darkness? She'd hardly ever used a phone. Maybe someone had left a flashlight.

She reached under the rickety wooden shelf and found a plastic bag. She unwrapped a flashlight, and the soft glow illuminated the circular phone numbers. She took off her mitten to dial.

An English woman answered. "911. What is your emergency?"

"My grandma fell. Her leg might be broken."

"Is she breathing?"

"I don't know. I didn't see her. My grandfather sent me."

"Are you near her now?"

"No, I'm not at the house. I'm calling from the community phone shack."

"Are you Amish?"

"Yah."

"Can you give me the address where your grandmother is?"

Susie gave her the address, and the voice said, "Thank you. I have an ambulance on the way."

She hung up and leaned against the thin wall of the phone shack, trembling. She had run too fast, but there had been a pressing need.

Susie couldn't imagine what Grandma had been doing outside at this hour of the morning and in this weather. Grandpa hadn't said. Had she been sleepwalking? Was Grandma ill and perhaps had been wandering? How bad must the injury be? Grandpa had been shaken to his core.

She opened the door of the phone shack and stepped outside. The wind hadn't let up, even with the first hint of dawn on the leaden horizon. A storm brewed in the west, sweeping in from the prairie. There would be snow, perhaps even a blizzard. What if Grandma had fallen when the roads were impassable?

Susie shivered and ran again. Wilma must be told. Wilma would wonder where she was this morning. Susie ran faster toward the bakery.

The distance between Wilma's heart and hers continued to grow each Sunday evening Amos drove her home from the hymn singing. She would lean against Amos's shoulder in the buggy and allow the sweetness of his strength to flow through her body. The closer she grew to the man, the further she moved from Wilma. They should be traveling together on this journey. Instead, a tempest was also brewing on the horizon of their hearts. Was this winter storm the first sign of its arrival?

She would lose Amos if Wilma couldn't find peace. Wilma was being asked to give up so much—the desire of her heart, her longing for a husband, the dream that had persevered in her mind. They had tried their best, and they had failed. Maybe she should refuse to date Amos again, despite Wilma's protests, until James came to his senses.

Susie stopped short as she approached the bakery door and burst inside. The place appeared empty.

"Wilma!" she called.

There was no answer. Wilma must have gone in search of her.

Susie rushed back to Grandpa's house. She had been gone long enough. Wilma would find her somehow. She slowed on the front porch and entered the house cautiously. Wilma was bent over Grandma's form on the couch, with Grandpa standing beside her.

"You called the English people?" Grandpa asked anxiously.

"Yah. The ambulance is on its way."

"Praise the Lord," Grandpa said.

"How is she?" Susie stepped closer. Grandma was propped up on pillows with her leg elevated. Susie could see it was swollen.

Wilma took Susie's elbow and led her away. "I am so sorry about this."

"It's not your fault."

"I was angry with you, thinking you had overslept. I'm losing my mind, and now Grandma is hurt."

Susie hugged her cousin tightly. Sirens sounded in the distance.

The two kneeled in front of Grandma. "The ambulance is coming," Susie told her.

Wilma held Grandma's hand. "What were you doing outside at this time of the morning?"

"Dumping the morning's ashes from the cookstove," Grandpa grumbled. "She should have called me."

Grandma grimaced. "I guess we don't want to admit our age, but I don't think I have any choice after this."

The family pressed close to each other as the ambulance pulled into the driveway.

That afternoon Charity stood at the door of her schoolhouse, smiling and waving to the departing students. They were growing close to her heart, especially James's sister Becky.

Becky raced around the edge of the schoolhouse. Her brother Samuel's buggy sat in the driveway, but Becky approached Charity instead. "Can I give you a hug goodbye?"

Charity opened her arms without hesitation, and the girl clung to her.

"You won't fall and break your leg tonight?" Becky's anxious face peered up at her.

She pushed the loose curls under Becky's small bonnet. "I hope not. I will be *very* careful."

Becky nodded, then ran over and hopped into her brother's buggy.

The news of Grandma Byler's fall had been brought to the schoolhouse by Deacon Jonas and had unsettled the whole day. Tomorrow would go better after the students had returned to the comfort of their homes. Life would go on, as it always did, and Grandma Byler would heal.

There would be bills to pay, and Grandpa Byler wasn't rich. There was no insurance. The community's traditions were firm. One trusted the Lord and His people to provide, instead of the English insurance companies. Grandpa Byler had done so much for her. Somehow she should help. But how? A parochial teacher's salary didn't go far. The few dollars she had to give wouldn't make a dent in the enormous hospital bill he would have to pay.

Was this winter going to be a time of trouble? At the moment it seemed so. She knew James would use the occasion to stop by the schoolhouse on his way home from work. He was expecting an answer from her. He wanted a regular dating schedule, an official one, instead of brief stops at the schoolhouse.

With a final wave, Charity began to close the schoolhouse door, but paused when a buggy appeared in the distance. She had guessed correctly, but James was early. Likely the threatening storm had cut into his working hours.

She retreated and waited while the hoofbeats came in the schoolhouse driveway. The knock soon followed.

"Come in."

James's smiling face appeared. "It's me again."

She returned his smile. "I'm here."

"I guess you heard the news?"

She nodded.

"Hard at work, I see." He moved closer, his gaze drifting over the papers on her desk. "Everyone getting passing grades?"

"Are you questioning my teaching abilities?"

He laughed. "No, simply the students' IQs."

She made a face at him. "They are all passing."

His face sobered. "Am I passing the grade? I'm beginning to wonder."

"James," she begged, "you know I need time."

"There will be talk soon," he said. "If I keep stopping by on my way home from work instead of dating you properly."

"You don't have to stop by."

"Can I take you home on Sunday evening? Please say yah."

"And if I say yah?"

His face lit up. "Then happiness and joy will fill my heart."

"I didn't mean that."

"Then what did you mean?"

Charity reached for his hand. "Okay. I'll let you bring me home, but that's as far as I can go. We can talk then. Respectably."

His fingers entwined in hers. "You don't know what this means to me."

She tugged on his hand. "I'm not what you think I am. I'm broken. I'm damaged goods. You should not waste your time on me."

"But you said yah." James glanced out the window. "I have to go. The storm is brewing, and the chores must be done early, but this is the greatest news—the greatest in all my life." Grinning, he hurried outside and waved out the door of the buggy until he turned onto the main road.

She watched him leave. Had she done the right thing? He had been so insistent. But to stir hope in a man's heart for what she could not give? Her love for David was alive and well.

She returned to her school papers lying on the desk with a sigh. She had been right. This was a winter of trouble.

14

The late-evening sunset hung on the horizon outside Deacon Jonas's kitchen window. Wilma washed a head of lettuce in the sink, surrounded by the murmur of the community's girls. Deacon Jonas's Frau, Ann, had invited the young people to dine at their house before the hymn singing began at seven thirty this Sunday evening.

Wilma shook the water from the head of lettuce and reached for the knife on the counter. The invitation hadn't carried the usual joy nor did her part in the supper preparation. Not since James's infatuation with Charity had taken hold of the man, coupled with her own failure to change his mind.

Abner peeked into the kitchen and winked at Wilma, then left.

These were not the first renewed attentions Abner had paid her. He was clearly emboldened by James's preoccupation with Charity. This morning at the church service Abner had caught her eye twice and sent warm smiles her way. She had yet to return them, but perhaps she should. Then James might notice what he was losing.

Abner wasn't a bad catch. She would have settled for him not that long ago before James had appeared. Abner had paid $700 at the school auction for two plates of sticky buns and the brief time she had spent eating them with him. James wouldn't even give her a smile anymore.

Ann directed the girls to place the food on the dining room table, cafeteria style.

Wilma hung back. She didn't want to show her face outside the kitchen. Abner would make his move when she did. His bold wink from the kitchen doorway had said as much. After her failure with James, Abner wouldn't expect a rejection when he sidled up to her in the line of girls.

"Let us offer the prayer of thanks," Deacon Jonas announced.

The conversations ceased.

Deacon Jonas prayed, then invited them to eat.

A girl tugged on Wilma's arm. "You coming?"

Wilma nodded and followed.

Sure enough, Abner sprang into action, falling in beside her.

The girl giggled but didn't say anything. Had Abner put her up to this?

"How are you tonight?" He leaned close to whisper.

Wilma gave him a slight smile.

He glowed. "Goot, it appears. How's your grandma?"

"Coming along. She'll be home tomorrow."

"Quite the hospital bill that will be." He made a face.

"I suppose so," Wilma allowed.

She hadn't thought about the expense of Grandma's care, other than the effort Susie and she would have to expend in addition to running the bakery. At least Grandma had fallen in the winter when the bakery was shut down for most of the week. They would have been overwhelmed in the summertime.

Abner filled his plate to the brim. "Can I sit with you?"

Wilma shrugged. Hopelessness swept over her.

He didn't appear to notice her despair. "Over there?" He didn't wait for an answer before leading the way to the back of the room.

Wilma lowered herself onto the chair beside him.

"This is quite the privilege, and I didn't have to pay a dime." Abner grinned. "We should do this more often."

She didn't respond. James had just walked up to Charity in the food line. Why did the man have to spoil this moment for her? She could at least have tried to enjoy her time with Abner if she hadn't seen that.

"He's quite taken with her," Abner said, obviously pleased with the observation.

"She can paint." Wilma couldn't keep the sharpness from her voice.

"You don't have to worry about your lack of painting skills." He took a big bite of food. "You can bake. That's better."

Wilma bit back a retort. Abner was not to blame for James's obsession with Charity.

She caught Abner's sideways glance. "What?"

"Are you available after the hymn singing tonight? I can take you home. At least give me that much. I'll drop you at the door."

"I can't. You know that."

"I *don't* know that. The competition has been thinned out considerably, if you ask me."

Wilma forced herself to meet his gaze. "Thank you for asking me to sit with you, but I can't."

"As in can't now or can't ever?"

"I need some time."

Abner looked disappointed. "At least it's not final. I can wait."

"Thank you," she whispered. "That is kind of you."

If Abner only knew . . . but he didn't have to know. Not ever. Once James was dating Charity for a long time, Wilma might accept a date from Abner, if he still waited for her.

"You are a sweet one," Abner said in a low voice.

"Someone will hear you," Wilma warned.

But when she glanced at him a second later, he appeared way too pleased with himself.

After the hymn singing that evening, Susie slipped out of the washroom door to find her way across the yard. A line of men hitched their horses to the buggies beside the barn. She lowered her head and found Amos's buggy close to the barn door.

"Goot evening," Amos said.

"Goot evening," she replied and helped him fasten the tug on her side before she hopped into the buggy.

Amos threw her the reins and jumped in, then accepted them back from her. With a whirl of wheels they rolled out of Deacon Jonas's driveway.

She clung to the buggy door. She still wasn't used to Amos's fast horse. Maybe she would never get used to him—or to Amos. She glanced at him in the darkness. "How was work this week?"

"The usual. It has slowed down with the storms. How is your grandma?"

"Okay, I think. She's coming home from the hospital tomorrow, and I'll take the first day. Grandpa will need someone there all the time to help with her."

"You'll be goot at that," he said with a smile. "You're goot at a lot of things."

Susie ducked her head at the praise. She would never get used to his kind words either. She leaned against his shoulder and allowed the joy to flow through her.

"James is taking Charity home tonight from the hymn singing," he said.

She sat bolt upright.

"This shouldn't be a surprise, surely?"

"No, I guess not . . . but still, it's a shock," she stammered.

"I know you had hopes for your cousin, but James is quite taken with Charity." His voice was warm. "Not that I can blame him. Charity is pretty, and she can paint. Not every Amish girl can do that."

Susie froze. Did Amos mean anything by his words? Had Charity bewitched him as well as his brother?

"Have you seen Charity's new painting?" he continued in the same tone. "The one with the pastoral scene based on the shepherd leading his sheep?"

"No, I haven't."

"You should," he said. "The woman is goot, but you already know that with the painting of the stallion on your bakery wall. Have you ever tried your hand at painting?"

Susie tried to breathe. Her chest was so tense she would suffocate soon.

"I did once in school," Amos continued, "with watercolors. What a mess." He chuckled.

"What teacher in an Amish school has the students paint with watercolors?" she demanded.

He glanced at her. "Don't you approve?"

"I-I mean, it's unusual. That's all."

He shrugged. "Maybe the Wisconsin Ordnung is a little liberal on the subject."

Susie hung on the side of the buggy as he took a corner without slowing down. The joy was gone, every last drop, and she wanted to jump out of the buggy. She had known that he liked Charity's paintings, but the admiration in his voice had not impacted her like this before.

"I wish James hadn't refused Wilma's attentions." Susie forced each word out, and they hung in the air like spears.

"Certainly your cousin Wilma will accept James's choice without a fuss."

"What is she supposed to do?"

"James has a right to make his own decision." He sounded puzzled. "Wilma having feelings for him doesn't place James under any obligation to her."

"I know that. I'm sorry I said anything."

"Charity's the perfect match for James's taste. I encouraged him to pursue her when he told me of his affections. You don't object, do you?"

"Wilma is my cousin. We are close. I want her to be happy."

"Yah, I know. But Wilma will be okay. She can set her Kapp for any man she wants."

Except your brother. The words almost slipped out.

He attempted a laugh. "I'm glad you're with me at least. Are you okay?"

"I'm fine," she said, but she avoided his gaze.

Charity opened the front door of her small apartment and lit the kerosene lamp, which she set on the kitchen table.

James waited by the door until the soft glow of light filled the room. He grinned from ear to ear. "My first date with the lovely and gracious Charity."

She hid her face in her hands. "Stop it. You don't know me."

His grin didn't fade. "You keep saying that, so maybe that's where we should start. Tell me what I don't know. There's nothing you can say that will change my opinion of you."

She seated herself on the couch and motioned for him to sit beside her.

"Unless you would rather wait until next time," he offered. "I'm perfectly willing to enjoy the evening with you shrouded in my ignorance."

"Don't tease," she scolded. "We have to talk. Things have come far enough without you knowing."

He reached for her hand. "What great secrets could you have? You paint, and I suppose that's mysterious."

"I was engaged to be married. We were in love, David and I, deeply and madly." The tears came, and she didn't try to hide them.

He squeezed her hand. "I had no idea you lost someone. I'm so sorry."

"David's not dead," Charity corrected him. "Not literally, anyway. He is dead in my heart, yah. But he lives."

"Did David do something awful? Is that why you are so troubled about this?"

"He broke up with me, not the other way around."

"Then you still have feelings for the man?"

"Yah! That's what I'm trying to tell you. I paint. David broke up with me over my painting—well, because I sold my paintings. It's awful." She twisted her hands in her lap. "We should not be talking about this."

Incomprehension filled his face. "David broke your engagement because you paint. I don't think I understand."

"David's Daett made him do it. Don't blame him. We had no choice."

James shook his head. "None of this makes sense."

"Yah, it does. I tainted Bishop Zook's Ordnung by selling my paintings. It might have been okay if the paintings hadn't brought in so much money. But someone complained—well, probably several people. David's Daett is a bishop, and he told David he couldn't marry us, not if I painted, and even if I stopped painting, that wasn't goot enough. Painters are always painters. My reputation was ruined. David suggested we leave the community or run away to get married in a liberal church, but I said no because that would have destroyed him."

"I can see that," he agreed. "So this is your great secret?"

"I'm so sorry. I tried to warn you, but the words never came out right." She again hid her face in both hands.

"Will David be back someday? See his mistake perhaps?"

"No!" She sat up straight. "He won't."

"It's okay." He reached for her hand again, and she didn't pull away. "I would never try to take David's place. Perhaps this can be a new start. Didn't the Lord lead you to this community?"

"And you love my paintings."

"This community doesn't object, and neither do I." He pulled out his white Sunday handkerchief and dabbed her eyes.

She clutched his hand. "Don't be so kind to me. I don't deserve any of this. I don't learn. I go right on painting even when it has destroyed my life."

"I wouldn't put it that way," he said. "I think some misguided people made the wrong choice. Your paintings are wunderbah. Thank the Lord you didn't give it up. Such talent is given to encourage and remind everyone of the Lord's tender ways."

"You break my heart." She sobbed into his handkerchief.

He patted her arm. "David must have loved you greatly."

She nodded. "He did."

"So where does that leave us?"

"I let you bring me home. Perhaps that is a start?"

"It is," he agreed with a smile.

"You're not angry with me?"

"Why would I be angry?"

"I just told you of my love for another man."

"The heart hangs on a long time. I don't hold that against you."

"But how is this to work?"

"We don't have to know," James said. "Just let me bring you home on Sunday evenings, and we will let time heal your heart."

"You would do that?"

"I would crawl on my hands and knees."

She choked out a laugh. "Your buggy is better, I think."

He joined in the laughter. "See, we are already making progress. You should not be alone. Loneliness can be a horrible thing."

"How do you know this?"

James shrugged. "Hearts were meant to walk hand in hand."

"No promises," she whispered.

"I need no promises at the moment." He opened his arms. "But may I have a hug before I go?"

She leaned against him, and they held each other tightly. His heart pounded steadily against her ear, as David's always had.

"You'll be okay," James finally told her.

"Thanks for being so kind to me." Charity followed him to the front door.

"Until next Sunday evening?"

She nodded, then watched through the front window until his buggy lights had disappeared from sight.

There was peace tonight. Was this the road back to healing and hope? With another man? The thought seemed almost sacrilege, yet she had thought it. James's strong arms had been around her, and she had held him close. Maybe time could heal the hole in her heart after all, even without David.

15

Wilma flung the dustpan down on the hardwood floor, and the sound echoed in the empty bedroom. Mamm and her sisters were busy on the floor below. She had volunteered to handle the upstairs Saturday cleaning alone.

She wanted to be alone. She was anyway. No one except Susie cared that James had taken Charity home from the hymn singing last Sunday evening and torn the last strings of hope from her heart. It was one thing when James had visited Charity secretly at her apartment, but this was the beginning of their journey to wedding vows.

She should accept a date from Abner. He knew what was going on and had already made his move. Abner was happy that James was out of the picture. But Abner could not understand that James had gotten into Wilma's heart, and she couldn't get rid of him. She couldn't block him out of her mind. Not if she had to see James smiling at Charity every Sunday morning at the church services. Before long, James would wave to the woman in the middle of the hymn singing. How could James be swept off his feet by a pretty face and a fancy English paintbrush?

Wilma shoved the broom under the bed and reached for the farthest corners. The straw bristles had cobwebs on them when she pulled the handle back. She plucked them off with her fingers and shook them into the wastebasket. They clung to her hand as if they had a life of their own. She grimaced and grabbed the wet cloth lying by the bedroom door to remove the offending particles. The webs vanished.

She stared at the cloth in her hand. This was exactly what she needed.

A cleansing of the web Charity had woven in the community. Like a spider, the girl had snuck in to hide in dark places. Charity had snared the best man in the community with her treachery. She would destroy James. Once married, the poor man couldn't get rid of his incompetent Frau. No Amish man could survive such a life. The spiderweb must be swept from the corner where Charity hid. But how? No one believed Wilma. They thought she was the jealous and jilted woman.

She gripped the broom handle with both hands. There was but one choice. The painting at the bakery must be destroyed. Why hadn't they done something about the awful thing before this? What if it hadn't been there those mornings when James sat right in front of her, eating her cinnamon rolls? Without the painting this might not have happened.

James didn't stop in at the bakery anymore, but she could do her part. Beyond that, who knew what would happen? Maybe there was still hope.

She had to visit the bakery this afternoon and throw the painting in the trash. Better yet, burn it! Watch the charm melt away as the spiderwebs had disappeared into her wet cloth.

She rushed about and swept the rest of the bedroom with long strokes of her broom. The next room received the same treatment, minus the dark corners. Any spiderwebs under the bed could wait until next Saturday. She finished with a flourish in the hallway. With the dustpan and broom in one hand, she flew down the stairs to the living room.

"Done?" Mamm asked her.

Wilma forced a smile. "I'm going down to the bakery."

"Did you forget something?" Concern filled Mamm's face.

"Yah, I did, but I'll be right back."

"You don't have to hurry," Mamm called after her. "The girls and I are caught up with the cleaning down here. Stop in and see how Grandma is doing."

"I'll do that." Wilma dashed out the front door. Now she had a handy excuse if someone met her on the road. Grandma did need a visit. She had taken her turn caring for Grandma on Wednesday, but she hadn't been back since. She should have stopped in on her way home on Friday, but the weekend ahead had clouded her mind. What girl wouldn't be troubled with what was going on?

At least Susie was dating Amos. That was the one bright spot in this storm. Maybe that was how James would come to his senses, seeing his brother date a decent girl who wouldn't starve him after the wedding. In the meantime, she would do what must be done.

Wilma burst through the bakery door and stopped short. "Susie, what are you doing here?"

Worry flickered on her cousin's face. "I'm . . . I didn't mean for you to come down. I can take care of the cleaning."

Wilma shook her head. "What cleaning? We finished last evening."

"I know but not too well. And you wanted to get home. I understand perfectly. I'm so sorry things are going the way they are. I'm dating one of the Troyer brothers when your heart is broken."

Wilma took a deep breath and settled into one of the chairs. She couldn't even clean properly anymore. Susie hadn't wanted to confront her directly. Mamm would have no such compunctions when she discovered spiderwebs under the beds at home.

"It's all the fault of that painting." Wilma pointed to it on the wall. "I'll help you clean, but first we have to deal with that thing. We have to burn it!"

"Burn the painting?" Susie had grown pale, and her broom clattered to the floor.

Susie's head spun. Wilma had burst into the bakery as if the place was on fire, catching her red-handed doing the proper cleaning she hadn't dared insist on doing last night. Susie bent over to pick up the broom and reached for the counter to steady herself.

"Yes, we must burn the painting," Wilma repeated. "There is no other choice."

"But Grandpa owns the painting."

"That doesn't matter anymore. We can't stop Charity from destroying James's life, but we can get Charity out of our bakery."

"But this is wrong."

"You're not going to stick up for her, are you?"

"No. I would never be against you."

"So let's burn the painting, and with my head cleared of that awful girl's presence, I can help you clean the bakery properly. Then we can stop in and see Grandma on the way home."

"You should think about this," Susie warned.

But Wilma already had the matches in her hand and was making a beeline for the far wall. "Are you going to help me or not?"

"What if Amos finds out about this?" Susie tried again. "James is enamored with Charity, and this is her painting."

Wilma paused to glance over her shoulder. "This will be the first step out of this horrible mess. We should never have let the painting hang up there this long. We could have put the thing in the closet at least. If this wicked spiderweb hadn't been up on the wall when James was sitting here, he might still love me." She wrenched the painting from its nail. "Are you coming?"

Susie regretfully followed her cousin out the back door.

A few feet away, in the shelter of the bakery wall, Wilma paused to light a match. The flame flickered under the canvas for a second before the edge caught. The stallion reared mightily toward the sky, as if he felt his tail catch fire. The flames colored the hooves with blackness and crept upward to melt the glorious colors of the ground with the sky. Wilma hung on, holding the painting away from her, with the smoke rising heavenward in a long spiral. The stallion's majestic head was the last to vanish into the curling flames.

Wilma let it go. "There. The web is cleansed."

Susie tried to breathe. The wind blew the smoke into her eyes, and she wiped them with the back of her hand. What had they just done? Amos and James had admired Charity's abilities. Amos would discover that she had stood by while Wilma burned Charity's painting, and the destruction of Charity's handiwork would not be easily explained.

"What are we going to say when someone asks where the painting is?" Susie choked out.

Wilma coughed. "We'll say it's no longer there and laugh. What's there to explain? Paintings move around all the time. Come, let's get the cleaning done."

Susie rubbed the small pile of ashes into the snowbank with her shoe before she followed Wilma back inside.

Her cousin was already busy. Wilma jammed the broom into the crevasses under the counters with a vengeance.

Susie peered out the front window of the bakery and caught sight of a small girl running down the road with frequent glances over her shoulder. Had someone seen the smoke, or worse, noticed them while they burned the painting? Susie groaned under her breath. She already knew the deed could not be kept a secret. They would both pay dearly for this transgression.

She sighed as she filled a bucket with warm water and a dash of soap. She wiped the countertops with care. Bits of dough softened and gave way under her fingers. How had Wilma missed so much last evening?

"Here, I'll do that." Wilma tore the cloth from Susie's hands. "I can think now."

Only Wilma obviously couldn't. She missed things right in front of her eyes. Susie wondered if she should say something. Her body felt cold, and the flames flickered in front of her face, with the stallion's proud head vanishing into the smoke.

"We shouldn't have burned the painting," Susie whispered.

"Yah, we should have," Wilma retorted. "This is the beginning of breaking Charity's hold on our lives."

"Then why do I feel so awful?"

"You'll feel better after a while. I already do." Wilma raised a dust storm with her broom. Her cousin knew better than to sweep too vigorously with flour on the floor.

"I'll have to tell Amos someday," Susie croaked.

"This is our secret," Wilma said firmly. "No one needs to know."

Susie glanced at the empty space on the wall. "You expect to hide that?"

"It's gone, and that's it." Wilma swept with increased ferocity.

Susie imagined the look on Amos's face when he found out. Coldness crept down to her feet. Why had she not protested more? She should have grabbed the painting from Wilma's hands. She hadn't, because she felt guilty that she dated one of the Troyer brothers while Wilma's chosen suitor went off with another.

"We should go visit Grandma," Susie stated. "This is goot enough."

It wasn't, but Wilma gave in at once. She emptied the water into the sink and wrung out the washcloth with a feeble twist of her wrists. Wilma was obviously distracted, likely with the same stabs of guilt that ran through Susie's heart.

Wilma led the way out of the bakery, and Susie followed. They headed to Grandpa Byler's place and stopped short at the lane.

"It's Charity's buggy." Susie stated the obvious.

"I know." Wilma was frozen in place. "I'm not going in there, not while she is there."

Clearly they had not removed Charity's influence from their lives.

Wilma turned slowly, as if in a dream. "I'll see you tomorrow at the church services."

Susie hesitated in the middle of the road. What should she do? She couldn't go in, not with the memory of those awful flames curling around the stallion's head.

Finally she forced herself to walk away. The rift between the cousins and Charity Martin was at least understandable. Burning Charity's painting was not.

Grandpa Byler leaned back in his rocker to give Charity a big smile. "I'm glad you decided to visit us this afternoon. What an honor to have the community's teacher in our home."

"I'm the one who is honored by your kindness," Charity replied, then smiled at Grandma Byler, propped up with pillows on the couch. "I'm sorry about your fall. I hope you are getting along well."

"I am," Grandma Byler said. "As well as a woman my age does. There are plenty of grandchildren around to care for me." She smiled at a young girl peeking out from the kitchen. "Carmi is here today, and she will spend the night. We have no complaints."

"It must have been awful, lying outside in the cold after sliding down those steps." Charity shuddered.

"That was my own foolishness," Grandma Byler scoffed. "I deserved a few moments in the cold for my carelessness. Grandpa was right there, so I didn't suffer unduly."

"She takes things well." Grandpa Byler grinned. "But no more dumping of the ashes on winter mornings for Grandma!"

They chuckled together.

If Charity could grow old like this, still happy and in love with a man, she would be satisfied.

"I hear you have caught a young man's eye." Grandma beamed at her. "Congratulations."

Charity blushed and ducked her head. "It's not what you might think."

"Don't be running yourself down," Grandpa Byler told her. "You have our full support as you rebuild your life in our community."

Charity looked away. "I actually came to talk about something else, if you don't mind. There must be quite a large hospital bill from the accident. Maybe I can help."

"The community will step in," Grandpa Byler assured her. "You don't have to concern yourself."

"But I am part of the community," Charity insisted. "I have a new painting at my place, a pastoral scene. If you don't object, I would like to send it back to Holmes County to sell. My paintings used to bring a tidy sum." Her face blazed red. "I don't know how to say this properly, but I think this painting would sell well."

"I think I understand." Grandpa Byler nodded. "I have no objections, but you don't have to."

"I know, but I want to."

"We would be greatly honored by your gift then."

Both of them smiled at her.

A sob escaped her. "I'm sorry. You are the one who is hurt, and I'm blubbering."

"There are hurts of the heart that burn deeper than breaking a leg, dear," Grandma Byler said quietly.

The tears flowed, and Grandma Byler motioned for Charity to sit beside her on the couch. The elderly woman held her hand until Charity composed herself.

"I'm so sorry for making a scene. I really am." Charity wiped her eyes. "But now that I've fully embarrassed myself, I might as well say what else I would like to have done. Would you consider sending along the painting of the stallion you purchased at the school auction? The price would be even greater than the one the pastoral painting will bring. I'll gladly give both amounts to your hospital fund."

Grandma Byler patted Charity's hand. "That's perfectly fine. We'll do that, and we are the ones who are honored. Is that not right, Grandpa?"

The old man looked deeply touched. "I agree. I have no objections to the plan. This is so kind of you."

Charity shook her head. "I am the one who should thank you, but I must be going. I hope you are better soon." She stood and rushed out the front door. At least she had said what she wanted to say before her nerve gave out completely.

"Thanks for coming," Grandma Byler called after her.

16

Late the following week, Wilma slipped into the bakery and lit the lantern in the stillness of the predawn darkness. The glow of light filled the empty space on the far wall. She should replace the painting with something else, perhaps a quilt, but what sense did that make? The effort would only draw attention to what used to hang there.

She would not admit guilt over the painting's destruction, because she was not sorry. Charity had not been harmed, and Wilma had broken the woman's hold on her bakery. That was the first step, even if James still smiled at Charity on Sunday mornings, filling the whole living room of Deacon Jonas's home with the glow.

She shouldn't expect results too quickly. Amos had taken Susie home on Sunday evening as usual. She had her foot in the door, with Susie's perfect example of what a Frau should be right there under James's nose. The man would have to open his eyes eventually. Maybe Wilma would be dating Abner by then, and they would be even at least.

The door opened behind her, and Wilma whirled about.

"Goot morning," Grandpa greeted her.

"You are up early."

"Just the usual." He didn't smile. "Couldn't sleep, wondering about something, and hoping that I am wrong."

Wilma avoided a glance at the far wall. "Is Grandma not getting better? I thought she was doing okay when I helped out on Tuesday."

"That's not what I mean." Grandpa settled into a chair.

Susie walked in from the back room. "Grandpa!" She gave a nervous little laugh. "We won't have anything baked for a while yet."

"I'm not here for your baking." Grandpa gestured to the empty space on the wall. "Where is Charity's painting? I've heard rumors floating around the community, but I know how things can get exaggerated with the bad feelings between the two of you and Charity."

Wilma pasted on a smile. "Surely you didn't expect me to keep the painting up there forever, especially after Charity stole my boyfriend."

"Charity didn't steal anything from you." Grandpa gave her a steady gaze. "James has not said the marriage vows with you."

Wilma tossed her head. "Charity is not right for James, and you should know that. The woman can't even cook."

"Don't you think James can make up his own mind?"

"Charity has bewitched him."

"Come now," Grandpa chided. "Your attitude worries me, even more than taking Charity's painting off the wall and hiding it in your basement at home—which is where I assume you put it, since it's not in the bakery closet. Or perhaps you put it in your barn loft, hoping one of your brothers will run a pitchfork through it while he throws down the hay. But you've gone far enough. Where is the painting? I need it."

Wilma busied herself at the counter. She was not going to confess. Grandpa would get over the missing painting once he was through with his scolding.

"People are talking about a fire behind the bakery and the burning of a painting," Grandpa continued. "I can't believe that my granddaughter would do anything like that, so tell me where the painting is. I shouldn't have to remind you that girls often lose out in their pursuit of a man. I'm sorry that you were the one on the short end of the stick this time. I know that's difficult to accept, but James has chosen another girl, and that is his choice to make."

Wilma dropped an apron over her head and tied the strings. She had to keep moving. How did Grandpa know about the fire?

"It is time that you accept Charity as everyone else in the community has," Grandpa continued. "I expect your attitude to change at the next Sunday services. We need our cheerful Wilma back, instead of a girl who looks like her world has come to an end."

"It has ended," Wilma muttered.

Instead of responding, Grandpa faced Susie. "So how are you doing? Happy, I assume, since you are the winner of a Troyer brother's heart. Do you know where the painting is?"

When Susie didn't answer, Grandpa frowned at Wilma in concern. "I'm sorry. I shouldn't have said that. I didn't mean to hurt you."

"It's okay." Wilma forced the words. "I'm happy for Susie. Maybe James will come to his senses if he sees his brother dating a real woman."

"A real woman?" Grandpa stroked his beard. "You really are bitter about this."

"What do you expect? I have been humiliated in front of the whole community."

Grandpa didn't say anything for a long time. "Has pride taken root in your heart on account of your baking? Have the amazing talents the Lord gave you puffed you up? Do you think yourself better than Charity?"

"What good is painting to a man?" Wilma snapped. If she made a scene, perhaps Grandpa would forget about the painting.

Grandpa studied her. "There is such a thing as love. Have you forgotten that? When a man loves a woman, things like cooking don't matter as much."

Anger warmed Wilma's cold body. "That is an awful thing to say. So why do we bake, clean our homes, and take care of our families, if those things are not vital to our existence?"

"I didn't say our duties aren't important. Doubtless Charity can cook. I don't see her starving, and she lives by herself, but Charity can't bake like you can. That's not a reason for a man to keep from falling in love with her."

"James would be dating me right now if Charity were not in the community. I proved myself to him." Wilma waved her hand around the bakery. "James was impressed with me until he saw that horrible horse painting. You saw him sitting there admiring it. Don't you think that hurt? I worked so hard and fed him my best cinnamon rolls!"

Susie held her breath as Wilma's shouts echoed in the quiet bakery. It was early in the morning, but someone going past on the road could easily hear the racket and come running. Wilma was losing control of herself. No Amish girl conducted herself like this, no matter what her sorrow.

Grandpa's face was deeply troubled. "You are making quite a scene. Our women are taught to live quiet and peaceable lives."

"Yah, our women," Wilma shouted back. "They are supposed to cook, sew, and bake, and then this happens. Are you blind? Charity has woven her web of deceit right over everyone. Paintings have no value in the community. Charity should be sent home, but she goes out on Sunday evenings with the best man I have ever laid eyes on. Don't tell me I shouldn't be upset. I'm doing goot getting out of bed each morning, instead of crying my eyes out on my pillow every day."

"You have taken this too far." Grandpa's voice was gentle. "Our duties have value, but the Lord also gives us gifts, which are not duties. They are the pure joys, the glimpses of heaven, which we can savor after a hard day of toil on this earth. Charity has such a gift, and she opens our eyes to see the Lord's hand at work in creation. A woman with those talents has a place in our community and in the heart of a man. To say otherwise is to deny the beauty of the Lord, His glory, and His great and mighty works."

Silence filled the bakery. Wilma glared at the floor.

"Can't you see that?" Grandpa pleaded.

"I see a woman who is about to destroy James." Fire still filled Wilma's voice. "If a girl who could take care of James had won his heart, I would accept it—with regret, yah, but that is how things are. This is wrong. This is unfair, completely unfair!"

Grandpa rose from his chair with a sigh. "I'm not going to argue with you all morning. I'm keeping you girls from your work, and I shouldn't do that. We will talk more later. In the meantime, I will pray that the Lord softens your heart toward Charity. The woman has her sorrows, which you don't know. Charity deserves your respect. Now where is the painting? I will go pick it up at your house or in the barn loft if necessary." He attempted a chuckle. "I pray I am ahead of the pitchfork."

Wilma studiously poured milk into a measuring cup.

"Tell me where the painting is, Wilma." Grandpa's voice was firm.

Susie held her breath.

"Are the rumors true?" Grandpa rounded on Susie. "Are you involved in this?"

She couldn't meet his gaze.

Grandpa sat down again. "I can't say how much both of you have disappointed me. You are my granddaughters and close to my heart. I trusted you with this bakery, but you have let bitterness and envy consume your hearts. How did you destroy the painting?"

"We burned it," Wilma spat out. "Charity wove a web like a spider, and James is caught in its spell. I burned the painting web."

Horror showed on Grandpa's face. "How could you?"

"I'm not sorry." Wilma bit off the words.

Grandpa pushed himself up on unsteady feet. "Never did I think things would come to this, but I suppose I am partly to blame."

Susie shivered. Grandpa was taking blame for their actions?

"Charity offered to sell her shepherd painting back in Holmes County to raise funds for Grandma's hospital bill," Grandpa said. "She suggested that I do the same with the stallion painting. That's why I'm looking for it. We can live without the money, but someone saw you burning the painting behind the bakery, so there is no hiding this. That's how sin grows and infests everything in our lives."

Susie and Wilma remained silent.

"You must root this bitterness out of your heart, Wilma," Grandpa continued, "and the place to start is a full confession to Charity. This has gone far enough. I'm coming back this afternoon to watch the bakery. Let's say four o'clock. Charity will have sent her students home by then, and you and Susie can use my buggy to drive over and apologize to her."

"Do you think he means it?" Wilma whispered after Grandpa left.

Susie didn't answer. She knew as well as Wilma did that Grandpa meant every word.

"I'll do the talking," Susie offered. "I'll take the blame."

"I'm going to die," Wilma said. "That awful, awful woman!"

"It's okay. We shouldn't have done what we did, but we'll confess and get this behind us."

But the flame in Wilma's eyes still burned brightly.

Charity glanced out the schoolhouse window when a buggy pulled into the driveway. Who would be visiting after school hours? James visited her on Sunday evenings, and this wasn't his buggy anyway.

Wilma and Susie climbed out of the buggy, and Charity gasped. Had the cousins come to confront her over James and their dates? She had done nothing wrong. Surely the two wouldn't stoop so low.

Charity answered the door. "Goot afternoon."

"Could we come inside for a moment?" Susie asked.

She nodded and backed away from the door.

"We have come to confess something," Susie began. "I hope you can forgive us, but we have done something horrible. It involves Grandpa now, and we are sorry for what happened."

"Okay." Charity tried to smile. "I can most certainly forgive you, although what you might have done, I can't imagine."

"We burned your painting," Wilma deadpanned.

"My painting?" Charity's head whirled. "But I just saw it this morning in my apartment closet."

"Your painting of the horse at our bakery," Susie clarified.

"Oh." Comprehension dawned. "I'm sorry to hear that. I was hoping your grandfather could sell the stallion to help pay for their hospital bill."

"Yah, Grandpa told us," Wilma said. "We are sorry. Well, I am sorry, since it was mostly me. We should have controlled our outrage."

Charity stepped back. "I'm sorry about James. I really am. He and I—I mean, it's by no means a certain thing."

"We really are sorry about the painting," Susie repeated.

"I was only trying to help." Charity wrung her hands. "I hope you know that. You shouldn't have had to burn the painting." She gave a little laugh. "It only brought ten dollars at the school auction, while both of you raised at least six hundred apiece. That's impressive. I can't bake, but I want to help where I can, with the gifts that I do have."

"We understand," Susie assured her. "That's what we came to say."

Charity nodded. "Thank you."

Susie turned to go, but Wilma continued to glare at Charity.

"I'm sorry about James," Charity repeated.

Wilma spoke quickly. "What we did wasn't right, but you have to know that dating James isn't right either."

Charity winced. "I wouldn't disagree with you exactly, but he insisted."

"Then it is even worse than I imagined. You are toying with the man to keep him away from me."

"Wilma, come." Susie tugged on her cousin's arm. "We came to apologize, not to argue with Charity. She can date James if he wants to see her."

"It's still not right," Wilma declared between clenched teeth. "And I have the proof right here, straight out of Charity's mouth."

"Wilma!" Susie begged.

Charity gathered herself together. The courage seemed to rise from deep inside her. "Let me be clear. I didn't ask for James's attention, nor did I encourage him in any way. But I won't be rude to him. I did tell him no several times, but he persists. Beyond that, James is kind to me. He likes my paintings, and yah, I like his attentions, as any woman would."

"You told James no in order to lure him deeper into your web, you spider," Wilma spat. "That's how men react to women like you."

"Wilma!" Susie tried again.

But the die had been cast. "At least I have a gift that can be used for good."

"But you can't bake," Wilma shot back. "You'll starve the man. Why don't you do what is best for James and let me have him?"

Charity took a deep breath and calmed herself. "Okay, you are right. You probably have a point, but you aren't helping your cause. Wouldn't a dignified silence be more in order?"

"I will not be lectured by you of all people on how to behave properly," Wilma sneered.

"Then tell your grandpa I said that he could tell you my story. Not that I care what you think, Wilma, but for James's sake."

"You are not doing what is best for James!" Wilma shouted.

"Wilma." Susie pulled with both hands this time. "We have to go. I am sorry, Charity. Wilma isn't normally like this."

"I understand." Charity forced a smile. "Don't forget to ask your grandpa about me. It's important."

As the sound of their horse's hooves faded into the distance, Charity leaned against the wall. How had she dared speak up for herself like that and say those things about James? The words had poured out of her heart. James did deserve better than she could give him.

17

After the Sunday morning service, Wilma slipped through the crowded kitchen, balancing a plate of bread and a bowl of red beets on a tray. The sermons had been long this morning, and lunch was being served late. Wilma's head throbbed. She was certain Grandpa had been preaching straight at her.

"The anger of man works not the righteousness of God," Grandpa had thundered and expounded on the subject until after twelve o'clock. By the time the testimonies were given and the last hymn sung, the old clock in the living room corner ticked on the other side of twelve thirty.

People were also staring at her. Who could have seen her burn the painting? Grandpa hadn't told her. His task had been to correct her transgressions. Grandpa had tried, but with the horrible words she had spoken to Charity, she had slid even further down the hill. Grandpa would have preached until one o'clock if he'd known about that.

Wilma would not ask Grandpa for details of Charity's story. She already knew everything she needed to. A fancy woman with English ways had slipped into a peaceful community and stolen the best man's heart. Grandpa and everyone else might have fallen for Charity's charms, but she would not. The painting was burned. She had been forced to apologize, but she did not regret what she had done.

Breaking free of the crowded kitchen, she burst into the living room where the men's table was set up. The men were seated along the full length of the room, their heads bent over their sandwiches, beards bobbing in conversation. She had chosen to serve the married men's table because she didn't want to see James and his continued fawning over Charity. She had heard Charity offer to wait on the unmarried men's table set up in the basement. Poetic justice would be for Charity to trip on the steps and send her beets flying straight into James's lap. With red beet juice dripping from his Sunday shirt and pants, the man might awaken from the stupor he was in and save himself.

Wilma stopped at the table. "Anybody out of bread?"

"Over here." One of the bearded men waved his hand. "Our peanut butter bowls are also empty."

She rushed over to him. Three of the peanut butter bowls were empty. Two other girls worked with her today, but they were nowhere to be seen. After hearing whispers of her disgrace, they must be trying to avoid serving the table with her. Well, she would handle things herself.

"I'm so sorry," she told him, leaving the bread on the table. "I'll refill those at once."

He glanced at her plate. "You don't have any with you."

"I have beets." Wilma tried to smile.

He didn't appear amused.

"I'll be right back." She scurried off. She would have to navigate the crowded kitchen again with her tray still full. There was no place to safely set it down. Some small child raced by, hitting the edge of her tray and spilling beet juice across the living room floor. Then rumors about her leaving it there would circulate, in addition to the ones about the painting.

The women parted for her, a few with strange looks on their faces. She knew they were wondering why the beets were still on her tray. She set her face. Explanations would avail nothing. She should have taken the time to find a place for the bowls on the women's table or chosen a different table to serve.

She refilled her tray with peanut butter bowls. She almost tripped at the kitchen doorway but regained her balance in time. Back at the table, several men gave her tight smiles, but their impatience clearly showed. How had this happened? She was usually the model of efficiency.

She leaned between two of the men with a peanut butter bowl between her fingers. Halfway down the bowl slipped. Deacon Jonas's hands flailed, but he missed the unexpected object, and the bowl careened into his lap.

She gasped as everyone stared at her.

Deacon Jonas tried to cover for her, grinning and plunking down the offending bowl onto the table. His fingers dripped gooey peanut butter. "At least it wasn't beets," he quipped.

Laughter rippled along the table, but everyone was staring. Not since Ellie Yoder had spilled hot coffee on Wesley Stoll's shoulder last winter had a girl so disgraced herself waiting on the Sunday morning tables.

"Well, now we have a bowl of peanut butter," one of the men said, trying to laugh away the situation.

She made her hands work, meticulously transferring the remainder of the peanut butter bowls to the table without incident. Her two missing helpers reappeared, fussing over Deacon Jonas and handing him wet washcloths, so the deacon could clean the front of his shirt and wipe his hands.

"It's okay, girls," Deacon Jonas said, loud enough for Wilma to hear. "Accidents happen."

Wilma tried to smile, but her face was frozen. She would never live this down. Even this was Charity's fault. She turned to flee, but there was no refuge. The kitchen was filled with women, many of them peering out of the doorway, the whispers abuzz through the whole house.

She held her head high. She had to face this.

"Wilma." Grandpa motioned for her to approach. He was seated a few feet away at the end of the table.

She trudged over to him.

"I want you and Susie to come over this afternoon," he whispered. "We need to talk."

She stifled her protest. She had caused enough of a scene for one day.

"You will tell Susie," Grandpa said.

"Yah." Wilma moved away.

The crowd of women parted in the kitchen, their glances sympathetic at least. Her two helpers were still fussing over Deacon Jonas. The bread plates on the table were now empty, and that blame would also fall to her. Would this disaster ever end? On top of everything else, Grandpa planned to rebuke her further. What other reason was there for calling them to his house this afternoon?

A light touch fell on her arm, and Susie whispered in her ear, "I'm so sorry about what happened. I was upstairs, but Sharon told me the details. Oh, Wilma!"

"Grandpa wants us to come over this afternoon," Wilma whispered back.

Susie's horrified expression was all the confirmation she needed.

"Can you help me with the men's table? We are way behind."

Susie nodded and grabbed another plate.

At least Wilma still had one person on her side.

Susie fidgeted on Grandpa's living room couch that afternoon, with Wilma seated beside her, staring at the far wall. Wilma's face had lost some of its defiance, which might help soften Grandpa's planned lecture about Wilma's mishap at the men's table today. Grandma sat in her rocker and smiled at them, but Grandpa's face was stern. He would blame Wilma's clumsiness on her continued surly attitude after they had apologized to Charity.

"How did church go today?" Grandma asked. "I so miss worshipping with everyone on the Lord's Day."

"The preaching was goot, of course." She was not about to inform Grandma of Grandpa's late-running sermon or of Wilma's misfortunes. Someone else could spill those beans.

Grandpa studied them carefully, stroking his beard. "So, Wilma, why are you still upset after your apology to Charity? What is going on?"

"I was trying my best to serve the table. No one was helping me," Wilma said between clenched teeth. "Perhaps I rushed too much."

"You know there is more going on than that," Grandpa chided.

"You don't have to preach at me. Church is past."

Grandpa fell silent for a moment. "Maybe you have a point. I was thinking about how our talk went last week and about some other things. I could have said things better."

"It's okay," Wilma muttered, staring at the floor. "Can we go now?"

"How did your talk go with Charity last week?"

"Okay." Wilma lifted her head. "I told her I was sorry."

"I saw Charity this morning before the services started, and she asked me if I had told you her story. Why would Charity ask me that? Why didn't she tell you herself? You would have stayed and listened, wouldn't you?"

"You should have asked her what she meant," Wilma said, defiance inching its way back into her voice.

Grandpa leaned forward in his rocker. "What is going on? Did both of you apologize to Charity?"

"Aren't you being a little hard on the girls?" Grandma protested. "It's understandable that Wilma is upset that the man she wants is dating Charity."

Grandpa sighed. "I suppose I am, knowing that I am partly to blame for this mess. So maybe I should tell you about Charity, but I don't think that's wise until we get to the bottom of this. Something isn't right. What happened after you apologized to Charity?"

Wilma pressed her lips together and wouldn't reply.

Grandpa turned to Susie. "Maybe you can tell me."

"It's not my place to say," Susie told him quietly.

"So something did happen." Grandpa turned back to Wilma.

"Why can't anyone see what Charity is doing?" Wilma wailed. "She's destroying James and now me. Yet you are chewing *me* out."

"Charity is harming no one," Grandpa told her. "You are harming others—and yourself."

"How can you say that?" Wilma howled. "I was openly humiliated today in front of everyone. Deacon Jonas will never forget that. Peanut butter in his lap!"

"Peanut butter in Deacon Jonas's lap?" Grandma asked. "What happened?"

Wilma's answer was another howl.

Grandpa leaned forward to lay his hand on Wilma's arm. "This must stop. You have to let go of your anger."

Susie held her breath as Wilma glared at the wall.

Grandpa addressed Susie. "Maybe you can answer this. Why did you help burn the painting?"

Susie's thoughts swirled, but she found the words somewhere. "I know that what we did was wrong, and I did protest. But at the same time, I also understand Wilma's point of view. Charity does go against everything that we have been taught, but you seem to support her."

Grandpa looked more tired than she had ever seen him. "I freely admit my fault in this whole matter. I should have been honest from the start, about what was happening, about what I was trying to do."

"Now I'm confused," Susie said. "What were you trying to do with Charity?"

Grandpa appeared not to hear. "I should have told Charity's story sooner, without her prompting."

Wilma turned to stare at him.

"What was your plan for Charity?" Susie asked.

Grandpa faced them. "I really am sorry, but I guess it is time to correct that wrong. See, Charity was—and still is, I think—deeply in love with Bishop Zook's son back in Holmes County. His name is David. They dated for several years and were once engaged. Before they could get married, trouble erupted because of Charity's paintings. They began to sell at a high price in a local shop and acquired some fame for her. David's Daett took offense and refused to allow them to marry."

"As he should," Wilma muttered.

"On that you are wrong," Grandpa told her. "A girl's talents should not be held against her. Charity was given her gift of painting by the Lord, and it is not a threat to our people."

"Look what she is doing to our community," Wilma protested.

"Charity is doing nothing," Grandpa insisted. "Our reaction is causing the problem. James would have fallen for Charity whether the girl could paint or not."

Wilma's mouth worked soundlessly.

"That is true," Grandma agreed from her rocker. "Charity is a beautiful woman, inside and out."

Grandpa nodded. "So is Wilma, and Charity's heart is still back in Holmes County. I doubt if she will be dating James for long. Not if she told me to tell you her story. You are the one who has burned the bridges between James and yourself, to say nothing of Susie's chances with Amos."

"I am seeing Amos tonight," Susie spoke up. "I will make my apologies and explain this to him. Maybe things can be patched up between James and Wilma now that we know the full story."

Grandpa shook his head. "That will not work. I am disappointed in your attitude as much as I am with Wilma's willful actions. You should see the seriousness of what the two of you have done. This is not something that can be undone with a snap of your fingers. I haven't talked to Amos, but I would think he is understandably displeased if he has heard about the painting being burned, and I think he would think twice about taking a Frau who was involved in such a hateful act. These things cannot be hidden. How Charity was treated by Bishop Zook is a much worse offense than any danger her paintings brought us. But as I said, I share the blame. I should have said something sooner. I should have approached Bishop Zook directly back in Holmes County instead of avoiding the issue and hoping things would work out."

"Why are you blaming yourself?" Susie asked. "We are the ones who have caused the trouble."

"I am also at fault. I took it upon myself to help Charity, but I did it clumsily, exposing both of you to the raw emotions of this issue. I am truly sorry." A tear trickled down Grandpa's face. "But in the end, the community must change its attitude toward these things. We are rejecting the gifts of the Lord to our own detriment."

Susie stood to wrap her arms around Grandpa's neck. "Don't cry," she begged. "We are really sorry. I know that Wilma sees this too. We had no idea we were working against you."

Wilma stood and came to stand beside them. "Susie is right, and I will try to rethink this. I know my temper is not what it should be, but that doesn't excuse how I acted."

"My lovely granddaughters." He pulled them close. "May the Lord help us find a way to make this right."

After the hymn singing that evening, Charity slipped out of the washroom door and ran across the darkened yard. Why had Susie not been there? Wilma had also disappeared the moment the last note of the parting hymn was sung. Something was wrong with the cousins, and anything seemed possible after Wilma's harsh words to her last week.

One of the girls had whispered in her ear, "Is it true that Wilma and Susie burned your painting?"

When she had refused to respond, the girl had added, "Everyone is saying it."

"I'm not talking about my paintings," Charity had said and hurried into the living room. Someone had tattled on the cousins, but she was not to blame. If the news was out, maybe Amos had already terminated his relationship with Susie. That would explain her absence.

Charity slowed to catch her breath. James's low buggy lights were just ahead, and Amos was standing beside James's horse, deep in conversation with his brother.

She cleared her throat, and the two men turned.

"Charity!" James exclaimed. "We didn't mean to keep you waiting."

She tried to smile, but her face felt stiff.

"Goot evening, Charity," Amos muttered. He turned to walk quickly toward the barn.

James motioned to the buggy. "We're ready. Hop in."

Charity climbed up the step and settled on the seat. "I'm worried. Where is Susie?"

"So you noticed." James whirled his buggy out of the driveway.

"Did Amos break off their relationship because of my painting?"

"So it is true that they burned it?"

"I'd rather not discuss that," she told him.

"Amos didn't do anything yet," James said, his words dripping with meaning. "Susie sent word that she is taking care of her grandma tonight."

"Out of necessity?"

"You get the point," James said dryly. "The two are guilty, and your painting is smoke. Don't you care?"

Charity shrugged. "This is my fault really—me and my paintings. I never intended this kind of harm to come because of them. I am hopelessly doomed."

James grimaced. "Isn't that a little dramatic? If they burned your painting of the stallion, they are getting what they deserve. That is not your fault."

He slowed the horse for the turn into the schoolhouse driveway. He stopped by the hitching post, and Charity waited while he climbed down and tied his horse. She was halfway down the step when he returned and offered his hand.

"Thank you," she whispered. "That was kind of you."

He stayed by her side for the walk to the apartment door. She opened it and lit the kerosene lamp inside.

James had already settled on the living room couch when she joined him. His smile was gentle in the low, flickering light. "No more talk about burned paintings. I want to talk about us."

She blinked twice. "I still think I am to blame for this, so maybe we should talk about our relationship tonight."

"I didn't mean that." He reached for her hand. "I want to say what an honor it is to spend these few hours with you."

"They are enjoyable."

"I think of little but you during the week. I can't wait to be near you again and admire your lovely face."

"You shouldn't say those things," she protested. "I am not what you need, even if you think I am."

James studied her. "What do you find wrong with me? Tell me and I'll change."

"There is nothing wrong with you. I appreciate the attention and affection you show me. The Lord knows how much healing you have brought to my heart by your approval of my paintings. That a man—an Amish man—should find them delightful, even right and beautiful, is a balm to my soul."

"They are all that and more," he said. "And so are you."

Charity leaned against his shoulder and buried her face in his chest. "For that alone I should promise you everything—my love, my affections, my heart. But the truth is I still love David. I compare you to him all the time. That's not fair to you."

"I come out failing, I suppose."

"No you don't." Charity sat upright. "That's the problem, and why I am tempted to embrace the chance you are giving me, but I'll always know what could have been and wasn't."

"You would deny yourself love because of the past?" James asked. "Surely you can love me a little, if perhaps not as much at first, but love can grow."

"David isn't dating anyone. I tried to persuade myself that he was, but he isn't."

"How do you know this?"

"I just do."

"You would make a life decision based on a guess?"

"My heart tells me it is so," she said. "I know what we had. David wants us back together, but he's embarrassed for not standing up to his Daett."

"So you can't love me because of your memories?"

Charity took both of his hands in hers. "You need someone else as your Frau. Your fascination with me will end someday. I am different. I can't cook or bake."

"I don't care." His voice was fierce.

"But you would care. Paintings don't fix proper suppers. There will be housework and maybe Kinner—if the Lord grants them. I am different. Our hearts have not been through the fire. That is what we don't have."

"And you have this with David?"

Her eyes filled. "You don't know the half."

"You trust him?"

"I trust our love." Charity covered her face and sobbed.

"It's okay," James said quietly. "Perhaps I understand a little. You are a woman whose love any man would cherish. I envy David." When she didn't answer, he added, "I guess there is nothing that can be done."

"There is not," she agreed.

"I blame this all on Wilma and Susie." His voice was bitter.

"Please don't," she begged. "My heart would still belong to David even if they had not intervened."

James lingered a long time, sitting on the couch, holding her close, before he stood.

Charity followed him to the door.

"In parting?" Sorrow was written on his face, but he opened his arms.

She embraced him, and his fingers brushed her hair, tracing the long loose strands on her forehead. Then he disappeared into the night.

Charity picked up the lamp and carried it to the bedroom. Stillness crept through her whole body. Grandpa Byler had intended that she begin life anew in this community, but once more she had chosen her own way. If she was wrong, there would be no turning around in the narrow lane. She had reached for the best, for the stars. Usually those slipped from the grasp of men.

Charity blew out the lamp and changed in the darkness. She slid under the quilt and cried herself to sleep.

18

Wilma awoke before dawn in Grandpa's upstairs bedroom. She pushed back the quilt and crept over to the window, then parted the drapes and peered into the heavens. The stars twinkled overhead in a brilliant swath that swept up from the horizon.

"Was I too harsh with you girls?" Grandpa had asked when she arrived last night to take over for Susie.

Susie had bolted from the house without a response.

"You'll have to give us some time to figure this out," Wilma had told Grandpa. "I'm trying to do my part, but my heart is still in turmoil."

She had gotten Susie into the mess, and somehow she must be the one to alleviate the problem. James's affections for her couldn't be salvaged—if indeed they had ever existed—but perhaps Amos could be reconciled with Susie.

At the moment, any effort seemed too much. Her temper had hurt both Grandpa and Susie. Her misunderstanding of Charity's motives had led to her fumbling the peanut butter bowl, which had sailed into Deacon Jonas's lap. She still felt numb from that embarrassment. The image would remain in the community's mind for years. The story would be retold to people's great-grandchildren.

Wilma turned away from the window. She lit the kerosene lamp and dressed, taking the light with her as she slowly descended the stairs. Each step squawked in protest. Her grandparents would awaken, if they weren't already out of bed. Wilma cracked open the stair door. There was a soft glow of light coming from the bedroom hallway.

She stepped down and called, "Do you need anything, Grandma?"

The muffled answer came back, "No, dear. Grandpa just brought me a glass of water."

Wilma retreated to the kitchen, and footsteps soon followed. "How is Grandma?" she asked without turning around.

"Quite well, with the loving care of so many helping hands." The chair squeaked as Grandpa sat down. "I told Susie it wasn't wise that she stayed home from the hymn singing last night, but she told me she couldn't face Amos."

"I agree." Wilma turned to him. "We are trying our best to find a way out of this mess."

Grandpa sighed. "Did you sleep well?"

She rubbed her forehead. "I think I did."

"Headache?" Grandpa lifted his bushy eyebrows.

"No. Just thinking."

"I've been praying for you."

Wilma looked away.

"Is the anger still in your heart?"

"I'm trying," she whispered.

Grandpa nodded. "I feel terrible that you girls became so deeply entangled in my venture."

She twisted her fingers. "I'm sorry that I made things worse. I was sure our old-fashioned ways would win."

"There's nothing wrong with our old-fashioned ways. I never intended that lesson."

"I know you didn't. I guess I misunderstood."

"I don't blame you. I blame myself."

"You shouldn't," she protested. "But do you really think there's room for me and Charity in the same community? I mean, the feelings between us are pretty bad."

"I know there is!" Grandpa was emphatic. "I will help where I can to make this right. I don't regret reaching out to Charity, only in how I handled things. I should have been open with you girls from the start, especially after I hung the painting in your bakery."

"Your bakery," Wilma reminded him, "and you are not to blame."

"I know what I know. I am at fault, but I pray the Lord will show us a way forward."

Wilma sighed. "I can never win James back."

"You'll have to leave that in the Lord's hands."

"But I still want him."

"What we want is not always what is best for us. For the time being I think we should focus on helping Charity. The girl is in a lot of pain and so is David. If there ever was a tragedy, it's those two."

"You want me to help Charity?"

"Can you? Include her in things when there are youth gatherings?"

Wilma took a deep breath. Her chest throbbed. "Maybe I can try. We have not exactly seen eye to eye since she moved into the community."

"I know the road is difficult," Grandpa comforted her. "I wish I could do more to help."

"If I could believe there was hope for me and James, it would help. Now it's like having my heart ripped out again."

His face grew sorrowful. "Yet we must often proceed with what is right without promises of a guaranteed result. The Lord will certainly help us."

She lit the cookstove and set a pan over the flame. "I'm fixing breakfast. Hopefully I still know how."

"You will always be one of the best cooks in the community. Nothing will change that. The Lord wishes only to add virtue to your life through this trial."

She added butter to the pan and cracked in the eggs. She glanced at Grandpa. "I know what you said, but if James ever loves me, I can take anything."

He came over to stand beside her and slipped his arm around her shoulders. "You will always be my dear granddaughter. I love you with all my heart, but you must let James go. I know that's difficult to hear, but healing cannot come any other way. While we hold on, the Lord's work is hindered."

"What if James never loves me?"

"Then you will come to see that this was for the best."

"I'll never see that!" Wilma wailed.

"You must." He was firm. "You have already come a long way, as have I. The Lord will carry us now."

Mechanically she turned the eggs over in the frying pan. "There won't be much for breakfast—eggs and toast. I hope you don't mind. It's all I'm capable of at the moment."

"That is enough," he told her, and his footsteps faded into the living room, where his rocker creaked as he sat down.

She allowed the tears to flow. She had lost James and could do nothing about it. Grandpa was right about letting go, but that didn't soothe the agony gripping her heart.

Dawn was faint on the horizon when Susie entered the bakery. In the silence of the morning, she paused. The emptiness of the far wall stared at her. What she wouldn't give to see the painting of the stallion there this morning. She should have stopped Wilma that day.

They had been so wrong about Charity and about everything else. So much harm had been done, and now Amos was gone. She had been a coward as usual, unable to face the conflict. Avoiding Amos last night had only made her nightmares worse. Grandpa had been right, but she had been unable to force herself to attend the hymn singing. After Wilma relieved her, she had tossed and turned in bed, haunted by the words Amos would say when he saw her again. Amos would know that staying with Grandma had not been a necessity but an excuse.

Susie pulled out a chair and sat down. Not that long ago Amos had been seated at this very spot, eating their baked delicacies and admiring the painting of the stallion. She should not have taken offense. She should have insisted that Wilma calm down. If she had stood up to her cousin, Amos would still be her boyfriend and her grandparents would have additional funds to pay the hospital bill. They had no one to blame but themselves. She should have known that their actions would eventually be exposed, even if that little girl hadn't passed by on the road and seen the smoke rising. No one could fault the girl for her curiosity when she peeked around the corner of the bakery and saw them burning the painting.

Susie jumped when the bakery door opened behind her. She whirled about to see Amos standing at the threshold.

"Goot morning," he said, but his eyes didn't smile.

"We're not baking today," she said, her stomach in knots. "Wilma is taking care of Grandma. We only bake on weekends during the winter."

"Then why are you here at this hour of the morning?"

"The sun was coming up." She tried for a light tone.

"Why did you call off our date on Sunday night?"

"I was at Grandma's house. I sent word with my cousin Nancy."

"I know that, but why? I want to know."

"I needed time to think."

He stepped closer. "I believe you're running away from what I will say to you about the burning of Charity's painting."

She forced herself to breathe.

"You and Wilma did burn the painting?"

"Yah, but we have apologized."

"And that takes care of the problem?"

"No." She hung her head. "That's why I didn't know what to say. I don't want to lose you."

"Lose me?"

She had already lost him. That was plain enough from the look on his face. "I'm sorry, Amos. I really am."

He stared at the empty space on the wall. "How could you burn such beauty, such talent? James loves Charity. He thinks the world of her, but Charity has called off their relationship because of what happened. What is wrong with you and Wilma? You burn everything in your path."

Susie stared at her feet. Her worst nightmare was unfolding.

"You know we can't go on with our relationship. I am at least man enough to visit and tell you."

"I understand." She forced herself to meet his gaze. "We have both apologized to Charity and to Grandpa. What else can we do?"

"It didn't sound like much of an apology. Even if it had been sincere, this will take more than an apology," he said. "James is heartbroken. If this hadn't happened, he might have been able to win Charity's heart and help her heal."

She pleaded with her eyes. "We're trying to do better. Both of us. We have learned our lesson."

"Why did you have to go along with your cousin? You could have stood up to her."

"We always do things together," Susie said, knowing how weak the words sounded even as she said them. "But, yah, I could have. I should have. I am deeply sorry."

Amos sighed. "Okay. If you promise to stop working with Wilma at the bakery and put some distance between the two of you, maybe I would reconsider our relationship."

Her heart pounded. This was her out, but she couldn't abandon Wilma. Nothing goot would come from that. "I can't do as you ask."

A look of sadness crossed his face. "I'm sorry to hear that."

"I couldn't go on knowing there was a rift between Wilma and me."

"So you like her more than you do me?"

Susie covered her face in her hands and groaned. "I can't put into words what you have come to mean to me, but it would be dishonest. It would be avoiding my problem again. I have to stop running away from things."

"That's admirable, I guess," Amos muttered. "But in the meantime I won't be taking you home from the hymn singing. Have a goot morning." And he was gone.

She staggered over to a chair with her hands outstretched. She sat down as weakness flooded through her. He wasn't coming back.

She had lost Amos.

After her schoolchildren were dismissed that afternoon, Charity harnessed her horse to the buggy and drove toward Grandpa Byler's place. She needed to speak with him and confess that she had failed. Nothing could be changed, but the words would settle her conscience, and Grandpa would understand. Somehow he always did.

She waved at a passing buggy. The parents of one of her students smiled and waved back. She hung on to the reins and turned into Grandpa Byler's driveway. Another buggy was parked near the barn, but visitors came and went constantly. She could chat with Grandma and wait until the others left.

Charity tied her horse at the hitching post, then went up to the house and knocked on the door.

Grandpa Byler opened it with a smile. "Charity. How was school today?"

"Goot. Thank you. And how is Grandma Byler?"

"Getting better quickly with all the attention we are getting." He chuckled. "I suppose old people need lots of attention."

"Speak for yourself," Grandma Byler called from inside.

His smile grew. "She's getting better, you see."

She hesitated. "Is it okay if I come inside? You have visitors?"

"Just Wilma, and she's getting ready to leave."

She paled. "I didn't know Wilma was here. I didn't mean to intrude."

Grandpa Byler sobered. "This might be the Lord's doing. Come in, and I will call her."

Charity stayed near the door until Grandma Byler motioned for her to sit on the couch.

The elderly woman smiled at her. "I am hearing nothing but goot things about your teaching."

"You are too kind."

"Your reputation is well deserved," Grandma Byler continued. "I want to thank you again for helping with our hospital bill."

"You are welcome," she whispered.

Grandpa Byler reappeared with Wilma in tow. He motioned for Wilma to sit beside Charity. "I just had an inspiration," he said. "I ran it past Wilma, and she has agreed."

Wilma gave a weak smile.

Grandpa beamed at Charity. "My suggestion is that Wilma gives you baking lessons, perhaps this afternoon yet, since their bakery is not in use."

Charity stared. "You would teach me?"

Wilma grimaced. "I have been wrong about you and caused a lot of injuries. If I can help in this way, why not? Of course, if you don't want me to, no offense is taken."

Charity's heart pounded. Did she dare? "But what if I'm not able to learn?"

Wilma laughed. "Everyone is able to learn. Everyone has to start somewhere."

"Says the person who is a natural!"

"You should take this chance," Grandpa Byler chided gently. "I'm sure Wilma will make learning easy."

"I don't doubt that," Charity said. "I'm just trying to absorb this."

"I'll get my coat." Wilma jumped up and left the room.

Grandma Byler reached over from her rocker to pat Charity on the arm. "You are brave to work with Wilma, and baking is really quite easy."

"I broke up with James on Sunday evening," Charity blurted out. "I came to tell you."

Grandma Byler clucked her tongue. "Such things do happen, and we wouldn't have wanted you to date a man you were uncomfortable with."

"Oh, there was nothing wrong with James," Charity said. "I was the problem. I wasn't able to love another man like I do David, no matter how hard I tried."

Grandpa Byler nodded gravely. "These are mysteries of the heart that only the Lord can understand. We said we would support you in whatever decision you made, and that has not changed."

Wilma reappeared to lead the way out the front door.

"Thanks for coming," Grandma Byler called after them. "To the both of you."

"I'm truly sorry about my temper and for burning the painting," Wilma admitted. "I hope you can forgive me."

"Did your grandpa have a hand in this change of heart?"

Wilma kept her gaze straight ahead. "Grandpa was trying to help you and David. I didn't know that."

Charity caught her breath. "I have to tell you. I quit dating James last night. I know I have disappointed your grandpa."

Wilma didn't slow her rapid pace. "I hope you didn't do that for me, because it won't do any goot. I've burned my bridges."

"I did it for my own reasons. I can't forget David."

Wilma didn't answer as she opened the bakery door and they entered. Then she tied on her apron and handed one to Charity. "Let's read the recipe together, and we can begin. You'll have a real cake in the oven in thirty minutes."

"I will?"

"You will," Wilma assured her. "If you can paint, you can bake a cake."

19

The stillness of the bakery wrapped itself around Wilma as she carried the plates of sticky buns between the countertop and the oven.

They shouldn't have made sticky buns for the skating party tonight, which was scheduled to occur behind the Troyers' barn. She had once gloried in the delicious pastries, but even Abner wouldn't attempt to sit with her tonight. At least not in public. Her reputation had fallen too low. She had lost everything except Susie and Grandpa. Helping Charity learn how to bake had brought momentary relief from the pain, but she was quickly engulfed again.

Wilma opened the oven door. The blast of heat swept over her face and dried the tears. She slid the tray in and set the timer.

"Are you okay?" Susie's concerned face appeared in front of her.

"Yah, I'm fine."

"We should talk about this."

"What goot will that do?"

Susie pursed her lips. "Talking always helps."

"The cinnamon rolls have risen," Wilma said, returning to the counter. "Time for the oven."

"They should wait another ten minutes."

Wilma paused in front of the pans. Susie was right. The yeast had yet to raise the cinnamon-laced dough to perfection.

"I can't even bake anymore." Wilma moaned.

Susie slipped an arm around her. "This has not all been our fault."

"You're just trying to make me feel better." Wilma eased herself into a chair.

"Perhaps," Susie allowed. "But it is true. Who would have thought that Charity's painting would be so well received in the community? We made an understandable, yet horrible, mistake."

"Fatal nonetheless."

"We both lost a lot, I agree, but life goes on. We can still bake, and the Lord will help us. Grandpa is also right on that point." Susie reached for her hand. "We should have been kinder to Charity, even if she was different." Her voice was low, barely registering in the silence of the bakery.

Wilma wanted to object, but Susie did have a point. "I was caught up in the passions of the moment, I guess."

Susie nodded. "Who wouldn't have been? We were on top of the world that evening at the school auction, and Charity wasn't."

Wilma shivered. "That does make things appear differently. How proud I was."

"I was right there with you."

"And you've stood with me ever since." Wilma squeezed Susie's hands. "What did Amos have to say when he came to the bakery on Monday morning?"

"The expected. That he couldn't go on dating me."

Wilma studied her cousin's face. "Amos must have known that I was mostly to blame."

Susie bit her lip.

"What did Amos tell you?" Wilma asked in alarm.

Susie attempted a smile. "It's okay. I bear plenty of the blame."

"You're not telling me everything."

"Let's focus on finding a way out of our problems."

"You will tell me the truth. I've had to face plenty of that already."

"Okay." Susie met her gaze. "Amos offered to continue our relationship if I stopped working at the bakery."

"And cut ties with me," Wilma guessed. "He did say that, right? The Troyer brothers hate me."

Susie's silence was enough of an answer.

Wilma gripped her cousin's shoulders. "You should have taken Amos up on this offer. Your life could have gone on."

"No! That would have been another mistake, and I am through with those. We are finishing this journey together."

"Is that why we are baking sticky buns and cinnamon rolls for the skating party instead of burying our heads in our pillows?"

Susie shrugged. "This is what we do. We can still bake."

Wilma frowned. "At the moment, baking almost makes me sick to my stomach."

"Perhaps we had best forget about the Troyer brothers."

"That is an awful thing to say."

"But the wise choice and really the only one. Grandpa would approve."

Wilma pulled herself together. "Sorry, I'm only thinking about me again. You were hurt as much as I was, and it was through my actions."

"I was by your side."

"But it was my idea."

"Yah, but what is the use in beating ourselves up? We did what we did, and even if we didn't, I would still have been what I am. Amos deserved to know."

"You mean, know what we were capable of?"

Susie nodded, the truth of the words like a slap in the face. She could bake, sew, and keep house with the best of the community's women. But she had been defined by the burning of a painting.

"We must find our way back," Susie said, her voice soft. "We can do what is right by doing what is best for Charity."

"I gave her a baking lesson on Monday afternoon."

"You did?" Surprise showed on Susie's face.

"Grandpa suggested it. I told Charity I was willing to give her further baking lessons if she wanted them."

"Then we are already on the road back."

"But where will this path lead?"

"I don't know."

Wilma's eyes lit. "What if it leads her back to David? Charity told me she terminated her relationship with James because of her continued love for David."

"We don't even know the man. How can we help?"

"But Grandpa does, and Grandpa knows David's Daett, the bishop."

"How could two girls change a bishop's mind?"

"We could offer our help to Grandpa. He might know."

Susie paled. "You think there is actually something we could do?"

"We could tell him our story. We could tell him how wrong we were."

Susie lowered herself onto a chair and stared at the far wall.

Wilma tried to breathe evenly. Was there no end to her humiliation? Telling their story would involve sitting on the couch of a popular Holmes County bishop and revealing her heart, her pride, her reveling in the community's approval, and her scorn of Charity. Word would trickle back to Nebraska, and the whispers would only get worse. Such things could not be kept secret.

"We should do this." Susie's touch was light on Wilma's arm. "But in the meantime, the cinnamon rolls."

Wilma leaped to her feet. The gooey goodness had overflowed the sides of the pan and reached halfway to the countertop. "They will look awful tonight. I have to find a way out of this mess."

"It will be dark, and no one will care," Susie said. "They will still taste good, if a little dry. But we'll add extra icing and I'm sure no one will notice."

Wilma buried her face in her apron.

The shadows had fallen along the Troyers' pond that evening, with a bonfire burning brightly at the far end. The flames shot skyward, illuminating most of the ice for the young people's first winter community skating party.

"Whoa there," Susie called to their horse, Midnight, as they bounced into the frozen field and parked.

Wilma sat beside her on the buggy seat, staring at the mesmerizing firelight. She had said little since their conversation at the bakery. They had worked in silence, finishing the sticky buns and the deformed cinnamon rolls, their contribution to the evening's events. There would be no praise for their baking tonight or exclamations of delight expressed around the bonfire. Those days were in the past.

"I want to go home," Wilma muttered.

"We have to face this," Susie said firmly. "It will only make things worse if we don't show up."

"At least our cinnamon rolls could have been done properly."

Susie jumped down and secured Midnight to a fence post.

Wilma lowered herself slowly to walk behind the buggy and open the flap. She filled her arms with plates of sticky buns. Not that long ago several girls would have arrived by now, offering to help carry the baked goods to the bonfire. Her face was grim. "We should go home."

Susie ignored the remark.

"They probably won't even eat them," Wilma said.

"You know they will. Things aren't that bad." Susie gathered up the cinnamon rolls.

Wilma followed her across the field. Several girls glanced up from the edge of the ice, busy tying their skates.

"Goot evening," Susie called to them, trying to sound cheerful.

"Goot evening," the chorus came back, but no one stirred from their task.

Susie deposited the cinnamon rolls beside the fire with the baked items others had brought.

"I'll go back and get our skates," Wilma whispered in her ear. She was gone before Susie could reply.

Susie waited, watching the sweeping forms on the ice. A few of the girls held hands, making their cautious way along the edge of the pond.

"We'll help you," several of the men teased them. "It's easy to learn."

"Like we are going to trust you," one of the girls replied.

"We are saints in human form," one man hollered.

"Meaning you'll have us flying in circles."

The laughter of the men confirmed their suspicion.

Susie's gaze shifted to a tall girl gliding gracefully down the center of the ice. The figure twirled, then dashed back toward the far reaches of the pond.

"Who is that?" one of the men asked, his voice laced with admiration.

She already knew the answer. No other girl in the community had such a tall figure. What would Wilma say when she came back and saw Charity on the ice? She might make good on her threat and leave. That would be a worse embarrassment than Charity's remarkable skating abilities.

"Let's see if we can skate like that," one of the men yelled, and the party followed Charity. The timid girls along the shore were obviously forgotten.

"Did you just see what she did?" Wilma whispered in her ear.

Susie's throat was too dry to speak, even if she had wished to.

"This problem is not going away," Wilma said. "We have to do something."

Susie still couldn't respond.

"We have to speak up for Charity in front of Bishop Zook," Wilma continued as she handed Susie her skates. "I have to drive this anger and ruin from my heart."

Susie sat down on the edge of the ice, her skates dangling from her hands.

"It's the only way," Wilma insisted.

"Whatever you think is best," Susie said quietly. "I'll support you."

Charity reached the far end of the pond, doing several circles, her skates light on the ice, before she swung to a halt. The freedom and exhilaration of ice-skating had always warmed her heart. Tonight, though, the joy wasn't there. She hadn't lost her abilities since last year's parties spent on the ice in Holmes County. What had changed was David being by her side. He matched her in skill, energy, and passion.

Her eyes stung, and she turned her face into the wind. Several of the men had followed her and were obviously trying to copy her moves on the ice. Usually laughter would have bubbled up at their antics. They were capable skaters, but none of them were equal to David. No man was, but she already knew that.

"Where did you learn to skate like that?" One of them stopped in front of her. "Race you across the ice," he added, not waiting for her answer.

"I'm not a match for that," she told him, forcing herself to sound cheerful.

"Do painting and figure skating go together?" another inquired.

"I don't know." She forced a laugh. "I just enjoy the fun."

A man bent low over the ice and raced toward them.

"James Troyer," one of the men muttered. "Should have known. The newcomers are putting us to shame."

"You can all skate quite well," she said.

"Where does he get those moves?" one man asked.

The group greeted James halfheartedly, then moved away.

Charity smiled as James whirled to a halt in front of her. "You're goot."

He tilted his head. "Why are you just standing there? Don't they skate in Holmes County?"

"Oh, a little."

He laughed. "You're trying to fool me."

"I almost did," she teased.

"But not quite. Am I as goot as David?"

Charity turned her face away.

"He was goot then?"

"Very goot."

"You're not reconsidering, are you?"

"Not really."

"I thought this evening might help."

"It's not you!" The words came out a cry. "I can't forget him."

"I wish we had met before you knew David. Things could have been different for us."

"Maybe."

James frowned. "Shall we skate?" He motioned to the leaping flames of the bonfire.

She took his hand, and together they moved across the ice. James let go and twirled her in a circle. There was no question he was goot, but he was not David.

James could never be David.

When they came to a stop near the fire, everyone stared at them.

“See, we belong together,” James whispered in her ear.

Any words she could think of got stuck in her throat.

20

Wilma fidgeted beside Susie, seated on Grandpa Byler's couch. They had requested the meeting this time—or rather Wilma had, after the ice-skating on Friday evening. Grandpa's Sunday morning sermon had convinced her even further that she was right.

Grandpa had given a vivid mental picture of the sheepfold, where the 100 sheep were sheltered from the elements, but in the count that evening one was missing. Grandpa hadn't looked at her or Susie while he spoke, but they must have crossed his mind. They had been the cozy ones, safe in everyone's opinion of them, while Grandpa had been the one who, like the Good Shepherd, had joined in the search for Charity's safe return to her community's good graces.

Grandpa settled into his rocker and regarded them with a somber gaze. "Surely there hasn't been new trouble between you two and Charity."

Wilma shook her head. "The reason I called the meeting is because I think we should make a trip to Holmes County and speak with David or his Daett. Perhaps we could change the bishop's mind once he hears of Charity's goot reputation in the community and how much she still loves David."

"You would do this?" Grandpa glanced between them, obviously puzzled at their boldness.

"If you will tell us how," Susie said. "We can't just show up at the bishop's house."

"If you ask me," Grandma chimed in, "this is the Lord's burden planted in these girls' hearts."

"What would you tell Bishop Zook?" Grandpa asked.

Wilma cringed. "Everything. The whole story."

Grandma gave them a sweet smile. "That takes great courage and boldness, but I believe it could accomplish what we have wanted since the beginning. Peace and healing for everyone."

"This is asking a lot of Wilma and Susie," Grandpa said. "Even if I had always hoped Charity would be fully restored."

"You are not asking us," Wilma reminded him. "We are offering."

"This is the right choice," Grandma said forcefully.

"I agree," Grandpa said. "I think I see the answer in this. But you have to tell the bishop the story from the beginning. Are you ready for that?"

"I am," Wilma said. "I have prepared myself."

"Bishop Zook is a kind man at heart," Grandpa admitted. "I think he made his choices under the burden of his duties and will reconsider. But what if he doesn't? Can you handle the fallout? He will not be quiet on the matter and will have an opinion about both of you. Perhaps I should accompany you on the trip?"

Wilma shook her head. "That would just raise the bishop's defenses even more." She took a moment to think. Maybe the day would never come when she would live down her rash decision to burn Charity's painting, but Bishop Zook's outrage would not make things worse for her. "We must do the right thing. My own heart needs healing too. I see no other way."

Grandpa nodded. "You have made a wise decision. From here the Lord will accomplish what is best. Other choices might have appeared easier, but they would only have led deeper into sorrow and heartache. For this I commend you. I will write a letter to Bishop Zook tomorrow, explaining my position on the matter and telling him of Charity's full acceptance by the community. I will confess that I didn't make the wisest choice either. I should have consulted him before we hired Charity as our schoolteacher so they could have attempted reconciliation."

Grandma smiled at the cousins from her rocker. "I am so happy that you have faced things and made the right choice. You can stay at your aunt Millie's place in Holmes County. I will write her a letter tomorrow and mail it ahead of your trip. Millie won't have to know the details, and she will not ask many questions."

"I'm sorry about the lost money for your hospital bill," Wilma told her. "I would repay you if I could."

Grandma clucked her tongue. "We will not cry over spilled milk. The hospital bill will be paid in the Lord's time."

"How much was the check for the painting Charity did sell?"

Grandma glanced at Grandpa and didn't answer.

From their silence, Wilma knew it was quite a bit of money—money that could have been doubled if not for her own anger. Her eyes filled. "I am so sorry. I feel absolutely awful."

"That you were willing to correct your ways is all we ask," Grandpa said. "The healing of broken hearts is worth more than money for a hospital bill."

"But it could have been done some other way," Wilma reasoned. "I didn't have to burn the painting."

"I suppose it could have," Grandpa allowed. "But you did destroy the painting, and as a result the way has opened for the restoration of Charity and David's relationship. I will not complain over the money. I have not done everything right on this matter either."

Grandma reached over to pat Grandpa on the arm. "You are a goot man."

Wilma stood. "We should be going. We have kept you from your Sunday afternoon naps."

Grandpa chuckled. "Two old people can nap anytime they wish. I am glad that both of you came."

"You do know where else you should be visiting this afternoon?" Grandma added.

Wilma shook her head as a chill ran up and down her spine. Who else must they confess to?

"Charity," Grandma said. "She must be told, so she can prepare her heart for what is to come."

Wilma stilled her protest.

"Thanks for your time," Susie told Grandpa with a warm smile. "And for your encouragement."

Grandpa stood and gave them each a hug, then followed them to the front door. "The Lord will go with you girls. I'll have that letter ready for you soon."

Susie drove her buggy into Charity's driveway and parked by the hitching rack. Wilma hadn't moved or spoken since they had left Grandpa's place.

Susie held on to the lines while Midnight switched his tail. "You okay?" Susie asked.

"I guess," Wilma croaked. "Will there be any bottom to our humiliation? Yet I must walk this road or I will go mad."

"I'll do the talking. You won't have to say anything."

Wilma nodded, and they climbed out of the buggy.

Charity appeared in her doorway with a puzzled frown on her face. "I didn't know you two gave baking lessons on a Sunday afternoon."

Susie tried to laugh. "We just came from Grandpa's house. Grandma suggested that we speak with you and tell you about our plans."

"Your plans?" Charity's confusion visibly turned to concern.

"Grandpa approves," Susie added quickly.

Charity's face relaxed, but her eyes were still worried.

"We want to tell you about where we are going," Wilma spoke up, her voice weak.

"We should discuss this inside then." Charity waited by the door while Susie tied Midnight to the hitching post. They walked in and seated themselves on the couch while Charity pulled up a chair.

Wilma cleared her throat. "Helping you learn how to bake isn't enough. The two of us are planning a trip to Holmes County sometime soon, once we can purchase the bus tickets and arrange things. Grandpa and a few of his other granddaughters will take care of the bakery while we are gone."

Charity stared at them. "Why are you going there?"

"We want to talk with David and his Daett," Susie replied.

Charity turned pale. "But why?"

"On your behalf," Wilma told her. "That is the least we can do for how we have acted. I know there is no promise of success, but I plan to tell Bishop Zook the whole story. I will hold nothing back."

Tears shimmered in Charity's eyes. "You would do this for me?"

"Burning your painting was wrong, and I'm ashamed of my anger and the things I said to you. I harmed not only you, but Grandpa." Wilma blinked repeatedly. "There is no way to make all that right, but I will do what I can."

"I can't ask this of you," Charity protested. "David and I have our own roads to travel."

"We have become a part of that journey," Susie said. "That is how community works. We are a part of you, a part of your life—yours and David's."

"You don't know David's Daett like I do," Charity said. "He will never give his consent to our marriage."

"Grandpa thinks Bishop Zook might reconsider," Wilma said.

"Even Grandpa Byler can't help," Charity whispered.

"Then you don't want us to go?"

Charity faltered. "I didn't say that, but you are offering a lot."

"We should go whether we think it will work or not," Susie said.

Wilma didn't hesitate. "We plan to go. Susie is right."

"I don't want you to make the trip because of me." Charity's voice trembled. "I don't deserve that kind of sacrifice."

"We are doing this because it is right." Susie kept her voice firm.

Doubt flickered on Charity's face. "If I hadn't been here in your community, both of you would be happily planning your wedding dates. Now if David's Daett rejects you and scorns your story . . ." Charity shivered. "I would never forgive myself for what the man might say about you. He'll think you are interfering, trying to change a bishop's opinion."

"We will have Grandpa's letter to explain," Susie said.

"We should be going." Wilma stood. "We are doing the right thing."

Charity opened the door for them, and Susie followed her cousin to the buggy. They climbed inside and pulled out of the driveway.

"Our courage must not fail us," Wilma whispered as the steady drum of Midnight's hooves beat on the pavement.

Susie didn't reply.

Charity paced the living room floor. Had she heard correctly, or was she dreaming? Wilma and Susie planned to visit Holmes County. They intended to speak with David and his Daett and attempt reconciliation. But that was impossible and foolish. She should have objected more firmly—unless Wilma was right.

She continued pacing. Did she dare hope that the effort would pay off? Was reconciliation the real reason for her move to the community? Could their engagement be reinstated? Could she be David's Frau come the next wedding season?

Charity grabbed the back of the couch to steady herself. If she swooned and hit her head, no one would find her anytime soon.

She held her head in both hands until the dizziness passed. She must think and not give in to despair. She must do something to help. But what? She couldn't travel to Holmes County with Wilma and Susie. She had her school duties, and David's Daett had forbidden her to contact either of them. She must stay here. She would wait and agonize without knowing what each morning would bring.

She lifted her head and paced the floor again. The painting of the stallion was gone, but the image had been branded in her mind. She could do better on a second try. She should have something ready for David if he did come. Something to show him what he meant to her—had always meant to her. If David didn't come, if David's Daett rejected the cousins' story, she would sell the painting and pay down more of Grandma Byler's hospital bill.

Charity opened the closet door and carried an empty frame into the center of the living room where the winter light crept in through the window.

"David," she whispered, "how I do love you."

She picked up the brush.

21

Wilma clutched the reins of Aunt Millie's horse as they trotted along the rolling highway north of Berlin, Ohio. Grandma had been right. Aunt Millie had given them a place to stay with a minimum of questions asked. Wilma's cheeks burned at the whispers that could yet make their rounds in this large Amish community. Why would two cousins from Orchard, Nebraska, visit the local Amish bishop's son uninvited?

"We won't be staying long," Wilma had muttered to her aunt when they had arrived late last night.

Aunt Millie had nodded and led them upstairs to their bedrooms.

"Is David Zook dating anyone?" Susie had asked.

"You girls came all the way to Holmes County and don't know?" Aunt Millie had scrutinized them for a second.

"Everyone sort of assumed, I guess," she had tried to explain.

Aunt Millie's face had darkened. "David won't date, dear. The man's heart was broken when his Daett broke up his relationship with Charity Martin. How you plan to change that, I have no desire to know, nor will I get involved."

With that their aunt had closed the bedroom door with a firm click. Aunt Millie was on their side, but patience would only be extended so far. Somehow they must succeed and succeed quickly.

"Whoa there." Wilma pulled back on the reins as a well-kept farm appeared over the next knoll.

"That must be Bishop Zook's place." Susie leaned forward on the buggy seat. "Aunt Millie said we should watch for the third place on the left, but she didn't mention the size of the farm."

"This outdoes even Holmes County standards," Wilma agreed. "Who is this David?"

The awe lingered as their horse trotted up the long lane. They parked near the huge white bank barn. Above them on a small knoll, the two-story farmhouse, with its wraparound porch, dwarfed them.

"What now?" Wilma whispered.

Susie didn't answer, climbing down from the buggy to stare.

Wilma followed and found the tie rope under the buggy seat. She had the horse secured when the limber frame of a young man appeared in the barn doorway. He studied them for a moment before approaching.

"David?" Wilma guessed. The man was handsome enough.

He shook his head. "Edwin. David's in the barn getting the team ready. We're cleaning out the barn today."

"I see." Wilma hesitated. "Could we speak with him?"

Edwin didn't move. "You must not be from around here. I can't remember meeting either of you before."

"We are not," Wilma said. "We're from Nebraska."

"Surely not from the community where Charity teaches." His stare had become intense.

"Yah," Wilma admitted. This was not a goot beginning for their vital errand.

Susie wasn't helping, apparently shocked into silence by the man's hostile attitude.

Edwin frowned. "Charity must have told you that our Daett does not approve of her and that she is forbidden to contact David. Or send someone for that matter." His eyes were like hot coals.

"She did not send us." Wilma kept her voice low.

The effort was obviously wasted, as Edwin stepped closer. "Then why are you here? You clearly know of Charity and the mischief she has caused. For your information, there is no hope of Daett changing his mind. My brother must be left to mourn in peace. His heart is already broken into a thousand pieces."

"We have a message from our bishop to your Daett." Wilma tried that angle.

Edwin's face flashed fire. "Then you *are* here to stir up trouble. Has Charity bewitched your bishop, along with everyone else in your community? Daett was right about the fatal attraction of her paintings."

"This is not true," Wilma protested.

"Then what is true?" Edwin glared.

"We need to speak with David and with your Daett." Wilma's voice trembled.

"You had best leave before anyone sees you," Edwin retorted.

Wilma met Edwin's gaze, but he didn't back down.

"Is that David?" Susie whispered by Wilma's side.

Wilma followed her cousin's point to the barn door.

Edwin also turned, but he didn't say anything.

The man who approached them had a rugged face, the features etched with sorrow. He was taller than his brother by a few inches and obviously older.

"What is this, Edwin?" he asked.

"They are leaving," his brother told him. "I was about to help them turn their horse around in the lane."

Wilma stepped forward. "We are not leaving. Are you David?"

He regarded her with the bluest of eyes, their gaze reaching deep into her soul. "Why does that matter?"

Wilma's lips moved, but no words came out. Her courage had abandoned her.

"We need to speak with you and your Daett," Susie croaked. "In private."

"Don't do this," Edwin warned. "They are nothing but trouble."

David turned to his brother. "Why are they trouble?"

Edwin reached out to lay his hand on David's shoulder. "You have suffered enough. You don't need to hear what these girls have to say."

"About what?"

"We came to speak about Charity," Susie said.

"Charity!" Light blazed in David's eyes. "You know her?"

"They come from Nebraska, and they know about you," Edwin snapped. "Of course they know her."

David ignored his brother's outburst and asked, "How is she doing?"

"She is well." Susie ducked her head. "Can we speak with you alone?"

Before David could answer, a man's voice thundered behind them, "What is this about?"

Wilma whirled around to find an elderly man facing them, his white beard flowing down his chest.

Edwin hurried up to him. "These girls are just leaving, Daett. Don't concern yourself with this."

"I want to hear what they have to say about Charity," David said firmly. "They are not leaving."

"Charity!" Bishop Zook thundered. "Charity has sent these girls?"

Wilma held up her hands. "Everybody listen! Charity didn't send us. We have come because we wanted to come, because of what we have done."

Everyone stared at her.

"I have a letter from our bishop." Wilma took a deep breath. "It will explain better than I can."

"A letter from Bishop Byler? He has a goot reputation, even if he hired Charity as the community's teacher. Small settlements get desperate at times." Bishop Zook held out his hand.

Wilma reached into her dress pocket and handed the envelope to him.

Bishop Zook ripped open the envelope and pulled out the letter. He read silently for long minutes while the others watched him. Finally he looked up. "Perhaps we should hear what these girls have to say. Come on up to the house."

What exactly did Grandpa write in that letter? The question raced through Susie's mind on the long walk to the farmhouse. Her hands shook, and Wilma's face had paled. Her cousin's courage had been great, even in the face of Bishop Zook's wrath. David walked silently behind them, and his brother Edwin disappeared into the barn.

Bishop Zook climbed the porch steps and held open the front door. He waved them inside.

Wilma led the way to the couch, and Susie took her place by her side. David took a chair across from them.

Bishop Zook settled into his rocker with a sigh. "So your grandpa tells me that you girls have a story. Let's hear it."

Wilma clasped and unclasped her hands. "It's a long story," she finally began, "and a painful one for me. I hope you can let me be honest about what happened since Charity came to our community."

The bishop nodded. "Honesty is the Lord's way. I have no objections."

Wilma took another deep breath. "The story began when Charity arrived in our community late last summer. I didn't like her from the start. I didn't know why, but I soon discovered what I thought was the reason."

"And that would be?" Bishop Zook leaned forward in his rocker.

"My younger sisters came home from school with tales of her painting and how impressed they were. At first I thought this must be some passing fancy, perhaps finger painting or hand drawings like we did in school. I soon learned, along with the rest of the community, that painting is Charity's great gift."

"That it is," David murmured.

Bishop Zook silenced him with a sharp glare and turned back to Wilma. "Continue."

"I also learned that Charity couldn't bake well. She brought a cake to the Sunday evening youth gathering made from a purchased cake mix."

Bishop Zook's face darkened, but he said nothing.

"My fears vanished at this discovery." Wilma shrugged. "Charity is a pretty girl, and the unmarried men had been paying her quite a bit of attention. I admit I felt she was a threat to my marriage prospects."

Bishop Zook scowled. "Vanity is not of the Lord. You should not have noticed such things."

"I know, but I did notice them. Things went downhill for Charity from there. Her complete humiliation occurred at our school auction last fall, where four plates of sticky buns that Susie and I had baked were purchased at considerable prices after we offered to eat them with the highest bidder."

Bishop Zook smiled. "That was resourceful. What price did these sticky buns bring?"

"Too much."

"A couple hundred dollars?" Bishop Zook ventured.

"We brought in $1,300 together," Susie said quietly.

Bishop Zook gaped at them, then remarked, "I take it Charity brought her latest cake from a mix, and things didn't go well for her."

"She brought a painting," Susie told him. "Grandpa bought it for only ten dollars."

David scooted forward on his seat. "Was this the pastoral picture that sold for over $2,000 in Berlin the other week?"

"It was not," Wilma said.

Bishop Zook glared at his son. "How do you know about that woman's paintings selling in Berlin?"

"I haven't forgotten Charity," David said, lifting his head high, "and I never will. Look how productive and successful she is with her art, on top of doing the Lord's work as a teacher."

Bishop Zook turned back to Wilma. "There must be more to this story than a painting that sold for ten dollars. Your grandfather would not have wasted my time with that tale."

"Charity is a success," David insisted. "She paints the things the Lord has made."

"And we don't put such things on canvases for the world to gawk at," Bishop Zook shot back. "What is highly esteemed before men is an abomination to the Lord. And it is a sin to make a profit from it."

David sighed and settled back in his chair.

Bishop Zook waved at Wilma, clearly irritated. "Continue with the story. This foolishness has already taken up too much of our time."

"Grandpa hung the painting on our bakery wall," Wilma said. "About that time a new family moved into our community, and I fell for the oldest brother, James. I set my heart on marrying him, but my plans began to unravel after he noticed Charity's painting."

Bishop Zook snorted. "Shame on him! But why would your grandfather buy that painting and hang it on your bakery wall?"

Wilma paused. "I thought maybe Grandpa explained that in his letter."

"He didn't." Bishop Zook studied Wilma's face.

"It doesn't matter what his reasons were," Wilma said. "I should have trusted Grandpa or asked him. Maybe he would have explained, but the truth is I didn't care. My anger at Charity and the attention James paid her painting consumed me."

Bishop Zook held up his hand. "If this is a tale of jealous lovers, there is no need to involve me."

"I burned the painting," Wilma announced.

Bishop Zook pulled back in his rocker. "Burning a painting is a little extreme, but that's not the point, right?"

"I don't know what Grandpa thinks is the point," Wilma admitted. "I only know that Charity and her paintings destroyed my world—or rather, I destroyed it out of anger and jealousy. I had a wunderbah reputation in our community with my baked goods. I had set my heart on a man, and he was impressed with me. Everything was going as it was supposed to. I was being rewarded for my faithfulness to the community's standards of hard work, duty, baking, keeping house, and looking forward to a future raising my own family."

"I see where this is going," Bishop Zook said. "You tell the story of a girl who is in love with a man and with the old ways of the community, who lashes out against another world that intrudes on hers. I understand where this is going."

"That's the world that Charity upset when James was more impressed with a woman's painting than he was with my hard work and dedication to our ways. He fell in love with a woman who baked cake mixes purchased at an English store." Wilma's voice broke.

Susie slipped her arm around Wilma's shoulder and pulled her close.

"You should not have pushed our guest so, Daett," David scolded.

Bishop Zook nodded. "I am sorry if it was difficult to tell your story. You did wrong in burning Charity's painting, but you are not the only one who has committed a great offense. Thank you both for your courage. I am sure the Lord will reward you someday with a husband who is an honor to you."

Susie helped Wilma to her feet.

The bishop motioned to the front door. "David will see you out, and then he and I will speak. When are you girls going back to Nebraska?"

"Monday morning early," Susie told him.

"I will see you at services on Sunday, but don't leave without speaking with David or me." Bishop Zook's smile was thin.

David held the front door and followed them to the buggy. He untied their horse and threw them the reins.

"What happened in there?" Wilma whispered.

"Let's not speak just yet," David replied in a low voice. "I will talk with you on Sunday."

After classes were dismissed, Charity set out walking down the small plowed back road.

An automobile approached, and she stood against the snowbank to wave as it crept past.

The elderly couple returned the greeting, but they were clearly confused by her presence, as if they couldn't understand what an Amish girl was doing out on foot in the middle of winter.

She didn't know either, but she had to go somewhere. Why had she agreed to Wilma and Susie's visit in Holmes County, let alone to them speaking with David and his Daett? What a fool's errand. Bishop Zook was committed to the Ordnung and to tradition. The pleas of two Amish girls would not sway his opinion.

She should have waited until reports drifted back to Holmes County of her newfound acceptance as the Nebraska community's schoolteacher. Perhaps with the passing of time, Bishop Zook's position might have softened. Now her only chance at reconciliation with David had been ruined. Why had she been so blind?

Charity walked south with the wind in her face. The shadows would soon fall across the prairie. Yet they could not block out the hope that had begun to stir in her heart.

There was also the unfinished painting of the stallion sitting in her living room. If David never came into her life again, if she was forever surrounded by snowy fields that were barren, cold, and useless, she could still paint. She could still speak of the beauty she saw in the world.

Charity turned and retraced her steps. The schoolhouse soon came into focus. She would light the lantern and finish the painting even if it took until the first light of dawn began to creep across the snowy landscape. She would say what she had to say.

The rest lay with God.

22

On Wednesday afternoon the following week, the bus slowed for another stop, its gears shifting ever lower in a now familiar cascade. Wilma stared out the window at the passing houses. A few people stood on the sidewalks, watching the bus pass, waiting to cross the street. Their lives continued as usual.

Wilma rested her forehead against the cool glass of the window. They would arrive back in Orchard, Nebraska, by this evening, and her life was still a mess. How was she supposed to begin again or restore the shattered pieces at her feet?

She glanced at David seated in front of them. He had been silent for most of the trip from Holmes County. That she had played a part in turning the heart of a bishop, in hopefully repairing David and Charity's relationship, should fill her heart with joy. Instead, a lump of dread sat in the pit of her stomach, weighing down her spirits into the depths of despair. She wanted nothing more than her own bed and a goot cry with her head buried in her pillow.

David turned around to face her. "Are we close?"

Wilma forced a smile and nodded. David wasn't asking because he wanted to know their physical location. He had his own burden. His Daett had relented, but there was a broken heart inside his chest, to say nothing of the task ahead of the man. He would have to restore his relationship with Charity. In the meantime, David owed Wilma and Susie an explanation of what had changed his Daett's mind. After the Sunday morning services in Holmes County,

David had only whispered, "I'm leaving with you for the trip back to Nebraska."

The bus stopped, and the doors swung open. Two young women climbed on, smiling and laughing, and sat down. The bus lurched into motion again.

Wilma leaned forward. "David."

David turned again, his face etched with weariness. "Yes?"

"I need to talk to you," she told him. "Can you trade places with Susie?"

Surprise filled his face.

"I don't bite," she said.

A hint of a smile flitted across his face, and he stood.

Susie exchanged her seat with him without further protest.

"I want to know why your Daett changed his mind."

David gazed out the bus window, his three-day stubble a shadow on his chin. "Daett saw himself in your burning of Charity's painting, in your rage, and in your defense of the old ways. It dawned on him that he had done much the same when he forbade our marriage and broke our engagement."

"Your Daett said this?"

David shrugged. "Something to that effect. He told me he was sorry and that he would do what he could to undo the damage. He said that if Charity is a faithful church member in Nebraska and a blessing to the community, he would no longer reject her as a daughter-in-law just because of her art."

"Then you have your Daett's blessing on your marriage?"

"I do."

"You are not happy about this?"

"I am, but I am also humiliated. I lost Charity. I let her leave the community when I should have stood by her side, even if it cost me my Daett's approval. What kind of man am I?"

"Your Daett might have excommunicated both of you. Could you have lived with that?"

"I should have been able to," David said. "Charity is worth any cost."

"She must not have thought so," Wilma guessed.

The look on his face was enough of an answer.

She smiled at him. "Listen to me. Charity is a special kind of person. Somehow I think she will understand."

"She is special," he agreed. "But I don't know if she will understand."

Wilma met his gaze. "She rejected a goot man named James Troyer, even when he fawned at her feet. I think she did that for you, even knowing she couldn't have you."

David studied his hands. "What is this James like?"

"Handsome, charming, and he was quite taken with Charity."

"I'm sorry for you. That must have hurt a lot."

"I don't blame James. I made my own mistakes."

"I can tell him what you did for us. I owe you that much."

"Please don't," Wilma begged. "Things are messed up enough already. I'm through with scheming and trying to impress James—or any man for that matter. My faults are well known back in the community now. I'll have to live them down in the Lord's good time."

"I will help where I can," he said. "And may the Lord reward you for what you have done."

Wilma forced a laugh. "You sound like your Daett."

A smile crept across his face. "What you and Susie have done will get out, whether I spread the news or not. Thank you—both of you."

Wilma turned her face to hide the tears that rushed down her cheeks.

Susie turned around in her seat at the sound of Wilma's soft sobs. David regarded her with a concerned expression. What had the two said that made Wilma weep as if her heart was breaking? Perhaps the explanation was simple. They were on the verge of exhaustion from the long bus trip home, not to mention their confrontation with Bishop Zook back in Holmes County. Sleeping on the bus, with only brief naps caught between the constant stops, had worn their bodies down.

"Is she okay?" Susie whispered.

"I think so," he said and faced Wilma. "Are you?"

Wilma nodded but didn't turn her gaze from the bus window.

"Have you let Charity know you are coming?" Susie ventured.

David shook his head. "I didn't dare. I must speak to her in person."

"I'm sure she will be thrilled to see you."

"I hope so," he said. "Our hearts have been torn, and I have failed her greatly."

"Charity is a wunderbah person. She loves you."

"You are kind to say that," he said. "Charity *is* an amazing person. That she should love me is a wonder."

"I'm sure she doesn't feel that way."

David didn't answer, apparently lost in his thoughts.

"You didn't date anyone else during this time. That says a lot," Susie remarked.

He smiled. "How could I? We're talking about Charity."

"Oh, you could have," Susie assured him. "Most men would have given up hope and moved on."

"I gave up hope," he said, "but I couldn't move on."

"Why didn't you leave your community with Charity? There must be a dozen churches in Holmes County willing to marry a young couple in that situation. And the excommunication might have been lifted eventually."

"I offered, but Charity rejected the idea."

"Because you didn't want to."

"I wanted to," he insisted.

"But not in your heart?"

"So it's that obvious."

"Charity must have noticed."

"She did, and I was the problem."

Susie leaned closer. "I don't agree, and I don't think Charity does either. You are on your way to see her, and she is still available."

"Thanks to the two of you."

"You object to our help because we are women?"

David's laugh was bitter. "No. Because it wasn't me who changed Daett's mind. His heart could have been turned back then. I knew it, and I came up short."

"You take too much on yourself. The credit goes to Grandpa, not us. Without him, none of this would have happened. You shouldn't feel badly."

"She'll always know that I wasn't the one who healed our relationship."

"I disagree," Susie insisted. "Charity's heart has always been yours, and always will be yours."

"May the Lord grant me that wish," he muttered and settled back into his seat.

Susie glanced at Wilma. Her cousin's eyes were finally dry, and she appeared to have collected herself.

"Charity was open to baking lessons. In fact, I already gave her one, and she did quite well." Wilma gave him a gentle smile. "She's getting ready for marriage. She wants to keep your home and care for you."

David's eyes widened. "Charity came to you for baking lessons?"

"Grandpa suggested it, and I agreed. I do know how to bake." Wilma's smile vanished. "I thought Amish men required those skills of the woman they married."

"Maybe I'm different."

"You might be," Wilma allowed. "But you like it that Charity is learning how to bake."

"I am Amish. I can't help it."

"Then why no concern earlier?"

"Maybe love is blind."

"You expect me to believe that?"

"Yah. We wouldn't have starved."

"You do love her."

"More than you can ever know," David said. "But the time I failed to fight for her will be there for her to remember forever."

"Maybe we should talk about something more cheerful," Wilma suggested. "Charity will think we dragged Mr. Thundercloud back from Holmes County."

A slight grin formed on his face. "You are right. Life goes on, even with my faults, and I am about to see the love of my life, after months thinking we would always be apart. Who would have thought this day would ever come?"

"Orchard is the next stop," Susie told them as the bus began to slow again.

David leaped to his feet, nearly slamming his head against the ceiling of the bus.

The two young women seated at the front pulled their gazes from their cell phones to stare.

"You're making a scene," Wilma warned.

David looked out the bus windows as they bounced to a halt in the small gas station parking lot. "Where's your grandfather?"

Susie glanced out the window too. Grandpa's horse and buggy were visible on the far side, with Grandpa standing by the wheel. She pointed. "He's right over there. I'm sure he'll be willing to take you straight to her."

Relief flickered on his face.

"Come," Susie said, and he followed her out of the bus and down the steps.

Grandpa Byler hurried toward them with his arms open wide. Susie and Wilma met him for a three-way hug.

"Ah, my dear granddaughters." He held them at arm's length. "You have come home again."

"We have a visitor with us." Susie motioned to David.

Grandpa approached David and held out his hand in greeting. "Welcome to Orchard, Nebraska. You must be David."

David clasped Grandpa's hand in both of his. "Thank you for everything. For the letter. For sending the girls to Holmes County. For persuading Daett."

"Ah." Grandpa smiled. "For that we must thank the Lord and His great mercies, but Charity is waiting for you back at the schoolhouse. Let's not keep her in torment any longer."

David's expression was grim as they loaded the suitcases into the buggy and climbed inside.

Grandpa clucked to his horse, and they trotted north out of town.

Charity stood in the schoolhouse doorway, watching the road. She had despaired so often, even given up hope. Her heart couldn't take much more.

"The bus should be in around four or five," Grandpa Byler had told her. "I will bring the girls here to tell us how it went."

She glanced at the painting uncovered behind her. The stallion reared toward the sky with his nostrils flared. She had outdone herself.

This painting was better than the one Wilma and Susie had destroyed. Last night she had rallied herself with the memory of David's rugged face, his wholesomeness, his embrace, and his strength. She'd made the last brushstrokes in the light of dawn while anguish gnawed at her heart.

Charity tried to breathe as a buggy came into view. What if they found her crumpled in a heap on the threshold? She gripped the doorframe with both hands.

The buggy turned into the school yard and parked at an odd angle. Her heart leaped as a familiar, beloved figure—one she had never dreamed she would see again—bounded from the buggy and raced toward her.

She wanted to dash forward to meet him, but her knees barely held her. She managed to step onto the porch and hold her arms out to him.

He swept her off her feet. He rained kisses on her face, and his voice broke in her ear. "Charity, I am so sorry. Can you ever forgive me?"

"Forgive you?" She focused on his face. She was overwhelmed, still unable to believe he was really here. "For what? There is nothing to forgive."

"But there is," David said. "I did not change Daett's mind. Wilma and Susie accomplished that."

"You blame yourself?"

"Yah, of course. I did nothing. I did not fight for you as I should have. What kind of man am I?"

Charity smiled. "Let me show you." She took his hand and led him inside to stand in front of the painting.

David studied the scene for a long time. "It is beautiful, as your paintings always are."

"What do you see?" she asked him.

He moved closer. "A stallion on the prairie, defying the elements, nature, everything."

"You are not seeing what I mean for you to see."

David frowned at her. "There is only a beautiful painting of a stallion."

Charity said nothing and waited as he studied it further.

He hesitated. "You—you see me as this horse?"

"I do," she said simply, "with all my heart. I painted this in my darkest hour, with only the memory of your face before me. This is what I have always thought of you, and what I always will think."

He turned and his eyes blazed. "I will never deserve you."

"Who truly deserves love?" Charity asked. "And yet you and I have it, just as God pours His love out on us."

David drew her close and held her tight, with the stallion reaching for the sky in front of them.

After a moment, he loosened his embrace and Charity saw Wilma and Susie standing off to the side. She met their gazes and smiled. "Thank you, both. I feel like I've gained so much this day. The man I love and a wonderful—spirited—extended family."

Wilma smiled.

"This is where I—we—belong." Charity squeezed David's hand.

"It is," Susie replied. "Right, Wilma?"

"Yah. I'm looking forward to our next baking lesson."

"I wouldn't miss it," Charity replied, her focus drifting back to David's face.

"So we should be going," Wilma said. She gave Susie a pointed look.

Grandpa Byler nodded. "I imagine you two probably have a lot of catching up to do. I look forward to seeing you both at church on Sunday." He climbed into the buggy with Wilma and Susie following close behind.

As they did, another buggy approached on the lane.

"Hello!" Amos called out in greeting.

Grandpa Byler tipped his head. "Hello, Amos."

"Say, I thought I might swing by the bakery tomorrow after work and pick up a few sticky buns." Amos pulled the buggy to a stop next to theirs, his gaze riveted on Susie. "Now that you're back, I was hoping you might save me one." He smiled. "Or two."

"I-I can do that," Susie stammered, feeling a blush creep up her cheeks.

"Goot. I've missed them." The meaning in his voice was clear. "I'll see you tomorrow."

Wilma elbowed Susie as Grandpa steered their buggy down the road.

"I'm sorry—" Susie began.

"You have nothing to be sorry for." Wilma hugged her. "I'm so happy for you. This is what you deserve."

"But so do you."

"I am content to wait. The Lord's timing is perfect, and I have faith that He will lead a goot man to me when the time is right. In the meantime, there are many sticky buns to be made!"

Susie chuckled. "And cinnamon rolls."

"And don't forget the Danish," Grandpa added with a wink, leading them safely home.